INNATE

A Chance Dawson Story
- Book 1 -

INNATE

ERIC CARTER

Cover illustration by Josh Tufts

INNATE

Copyright © 2020 by Eric Carter

This is a work of fiction. Names, places, characters, and incidents are either the product of the author's imagination or are used fictitiously, and any resemblance to any actual persons, living or dead, organizations, events, or locales is entirely coincidental.

Cover by Josh Tufts Edited by Sirah Jarocki

ISBN: 9781087940632

For Oliver, Peter, and Ira.

Never stop reading.

Chapter 1

Normal is three hours away. It's the last day of school, and I daydream of summer break. My treehouse. Steamy streets and woods. Sleeping in. It will all replace these stale, frigid classrooms. No more dodging classmates. Instead, I'll relax with my family, who love me. And I'll get better. I just need some rest and peace. And, I'll get better.

Ms. Porter says something, but I'm zoned out. I don't hear her. Nobody hears her. We don't need to. We haven't received meaningful work for three days. Why do we even come to school the final week?

An announcement interrupts my daydream: "Attention upper school students. All juniors and seniors immediately report to the gym. Important instructions will be given in ten minutes."

"Is Paul getting out early?" I worry. My older brother is my ride home. I don't need any stress now. I'm so close to summer. So close to normal. So close to better.

Ms. Porter's phone vibrates on her desk. She glances at a text message. She pops out of her seat and starts towards the classroom door. "I'll be right back, students. You may talk quietly. Just, stay in your seats, please."

The door closes. The class erupts. Stay in our seats? Seriously? It's the last day of school, and the teacher leaves a class of sixth graders alone. Almost everybody leaves their seats, or at least turns in them to find friends. A small group gathers in the back of the room to plan one last prank. Others throw spitballs at the ceiling. Most are content to chat with friends. Me? I keep to myself, as usual. I need to avoid attention for a few more hours, then everything will be fine.

Everything is fine. Just get to the end of the day, my mind assures my body.

I take some deep breaths and hope nobody notices my odd attention to breathing.

Stay calm. No episodes.

Can anyone tell that I'm getting nervous? I rub my thumbs against my palms, another trick Dr. Watt taught me for staying calm. I feel eyes turning to me. Is the whole class looking at me?

Ms. Porter returns. Thank goodness. She'll take the attention away from me. I expect a perturbed reprimand for the chaos that exploded after she left, but her face is empty. The switch from orderly classroom to end-of-year madhouse doesn't phase her. Something else holds her full attention.

"Class," she whimpers. She speaks so quietly. She's scared. I think I'm the only one who heard her. What is wrong?

She stands for a few more seconds and continues to look straight forward. What is she looking at? She seems to stare directly through the back wall as if she can see something in the next classroom.

I forget about my controlled breathing. My thumbs stop moving. My fists clench. Oh no. I feel my nerves heating up. What is going on?

"Class," she says, a little louder. Most students ignore her and remain lost in their personal conversations.

A blaring intercom saves Ms. Porter from two failed attempts to claim the class' attention. The emergency tone screams through the classroom. Everyone cups their hands over their ears. The class snaps to attention. We turn to Ms. Porter and wait for an explanation.

"Class," she starts again. "There has been an emergency, and we are going to leave school early today. Please walk to the cafeteria. Principal Stevens will instruct you how to get home."

As she finishes speaking, a strange noise floods the hallway outside our classroom. We all turn our eyes to the door, equally confused by the unfamiliar sound. I hear students swarming and moving towards the cafeteria. But there's something else. It sounds like marching. It *is* marching.

Soldiers are in the building.

The contrast of middle school voices against stomping military boots makes my stomach churn. What is going on?

I join my classmates in an uneasy dash for the door. We throw it open. The hallway scene stops us all in our tracks. Armed soldiers file through the hall, taking no notice of the growing confusion and fear among the scrambling students. They are on a mission, and nothing will interfere. But what type of military mission happens at a school? As more students pour into the hallway, the path to the cafeteria turns into a stampede.

I freeze, trapped in the confusion. I push my back against a wall and focus on breathing.

In, 2, 3, 4. Out, 2, 3, 4. You must stay calm.

My thumbs rub my palms raw. I can't afford an episode right now. I feel the pill in my pocket. Dr. Watt told me that if I feel an episode coming on, I can take the pill. It will stop the episode, but it will knock me out. I'll be asleep in minutes.

Falling asleep in the middle of an emergency evacuation is not the best way to avoid attention. Maybe I can slip back into the classroom and sleep while this blows over.

I consider taking the pill. But wait. Paul!

I need to find Paul, and we need to leave. We need to leave together.

An avalanche of students and military entangles everything in the hallway and carries it towards the cafeteria. Paul is in the gym, the opposite direction. I squeeze against the wall and fight against the traffic. I feel like one of those fish that swims upriver to lay eggs. It's nearly impossible to move against the hall's current. But, Paul. I have to get to Paul, no matter the difficulty.

Somehow, I make it to the end of the hallway. What will I see

4

outside? I peek my head out the door.

Students and teachers clamber all over the school grounds. If anybody had made it to the cafeteria, they didn't stay long. Some students run to the edge of campus. Others head to the parking lot where the upper school students park their cars. Even teachers are taking off. I scan the campus in between the parking lot and the gym. Principal Stevens catches my eye. He pleads with an upper school teacher to stay. The teacher pulls away from him and runs towards her car. Before she closes her car door, she turns and screams at Principal Stevens: "The parents need to know first!"

Principal Stevens drops his eyes and slumps his shoulders. I think he agrees with her, but he acts helpless to do anything about it. He turns and walks lifelessly back towards campus. My eyes rush ahead of him to the gym and stop at the gym doors. A dozen or so upper school students are coming through the gym's main doors in an orderly line. They stay silent, surrounded by soldiers. They are escorted to a bus. It isn't a school bus. It's unmarked, with blacked-out windows.

I look back to the line of students. I scan for Paul. My heart beats faster. I don't know anything about this line or this bus, but I don't want Paul in either one. My nerves prevent my eyes from focusing. I shake my head and start over at the beginning of the line. One of Paul's basketball teammates is first. Jake Cross, a state champion wrestler, stands behind him. Jane Simmons, our school track star, is behind Jake. A pattern emerges. A pattern that surely includes my brother. I lose control of my breathing, again.

My eyes rush through the line again and again and again. There he is. Paul holds himself like the rest of them: poised, silent, and ready. But ready for what? What don't my parents know about Paul and the others?

The student athletes move in procession towards the ominous blackened bus. Compared to the rampage unfolding across the rest of campus, the small plot between the gym and the unmarked bus exudes an eerie sense of order. The soldiers and the students are on the same page. They move with a shared sense of purpose. That small group of students has joined the soldiers' mission.

I don't understand that mission, but I can't let Paul join. I must get to him. I must get him out of there. I need my big brother. I drop my bookbag. I drop my breathing exercises. I drop my thoughts. And I run: I run towards Paul.

Chapter 2

I start crossing the schoolyard. The early summer heat has already scorched the grass which crunches under each step. The thick air weighs on my lungs as I fight to reach my brother and the others.

Soldiers see me coming. I'm still not even close. I keep running anyway. Their eyes zero in on me as I approach. My body tires. I keep running. The guards form a human wall between me and the line of older students. They look prepared for an enemy attack. I don't stand a chance.

"Stop!" one solider yells. I keep running.

"Stop, immediately!" he repeats. The united wall raises shields to reinforce their barricade.

I keep running.

I wouldn't breach their stronghold on my best day. And this isn't my best day. My body nears its breaking point from fear and exhaustion. My stride unravels into a stumble, and I scream, "Paul! Paul! Paul!"

My reckless effort ends with a crash into the armored barrier that separates me from Paul. I fall face-first onto the ground. Soldiers are hovering over me. I feel their sweat drip onto my neck. I roll over and look up. Three warrior faces jockey for position in front of me. They growl like attack dogs at the end of a chain.

I can see Paul. He has heard me. He turns and takes a step towards me. Two armed men grab Paul. They hold him back. Paul tries to yank his arms loose. He's a more formidable challenge than me. Additional soldiers abandon the other students for the sake of keeping Paul and me separated.

"Identify yourself!" the three soldiers yell at me. Each is eager to have his say. Dust puffs off the ground where I landed. I choke trying to catch my breath. I can't answer them. They continue to yell. One lunges at my face, only to be pulled back by another who wants an opportunity to shout.

"Identify yourself!"

"What are you doing here?"

"Who is Paul, and what do you want with him?"

They continue their hurried interrogation, their crouching bodies blocking out the midday sunlight. I can't escape their breath. It's humid and sulphurous. Each additional outburst pummels my face. I can't get a word in to explain myself. Stars explode in my immediate vision and blur the faces in front of me. I ignore the interrogators and yell, "Paul! We have to get out of here! Paul! Come here!"

The soldiers stop yelling. Maybe they had it out of their systems;

maybe they didn't know what to do with me. Afterall, they were trained to fight warriors, not children, especially weak, physically exhausted children like the one lying helplessly on the ground before them. They know they can't let me get to Paul. Keeping us separated isn't difficult. It's almost as if I am too easy of a captive for them. Each looks at me, then to each other, awash with confusion.

My lungs pump uncontrollably. My heart feels as if it will burst out of my chest. I start to go limp. Even if I had a plan, I can't do anything about it. I can't move another inch.

Paul pleads with the guards: "Ju...Just let me talk to him for a second," he says. "He's harmless. I promise. He isn't going to do anything crazy. It's my brother. I just need to say *goodbye*."

"Goodbye?" The word stings my eardrums. No, not goodbye. Goodbye isn't an option. My breath starts to recover. But my nerves return. I need Paul here. I don't know what's going on, but I need him with me.

"Paul!" I try to yell, with little success. My dry throat and mouth trap most of my voice. One guard holds out a warning hand. He doesn't touch me, but it's enough to keep me on the ground. My mind urges my body to get to its feet. My body refuses.

Paul continues to argue: "Look, just let me give him this letter. You can read it. It doesn't say anything that you don't want him to know. It says I'm going with you guys. Give me two minutes. That's all I need. Two minutes. He needs me to say goodbye.

He has…" Paul pauses. "Well, he has these problems, and stress makes it worse. He'll get a lot sicker if he doesn't know that I'm OK. Just let me tell him that I'm going to be OK. Let me tell him that I'm going because I want to go. That I'm going because the country needs me. Please!"

The soldiers loosen their grip on Paul, and he cautiously walks towards me. The few men that swarmed above me draw back. I feel slight relief at the sight of Paul's face. He reaches out his hand to pull me up.

"Chance, are you OK? Let me help you up." He pulls me off the ground. He's strong. My twelve year old body grows heavier everyday, but he can still scoop me up like a backpack. "Hey, calm down bud. I'm here." He hugs me close. My head buries into his chest. I weep. I can't control it. Tears break through my closed eyelids like a failed dam and turn my dusty checks into rivers of mud. I'm torn between safety and terror. I know this moment will end. It will end soon. And I don't know why. Paul presses his hands on my shoulders, gently removing himself from my clutching arms.

"Look bud, I'm fine. These guys, they're good guys." I look from side to side. We're surrounded by troops. "They need some of us to go with them. To help our country. There's some bad stuff out there, and they need our help. But it won't last long. They know what they're doing, and we're going to win."

"Win what?" I ask, fighting my sobs.

"Well, there are some people," Paul pauses and looks over his shoulder. He doesn't know what he's allowed to say. The soldiers look at him, expressionless. "There are some people that are trying to hurt our country. These guys don't want to let them do that. And they need my help. My help, and Jake and Jane, and the rest of us." Paul points towards the line of students. They are already ascending the steps into the bus.

"Why would they need you guys?" I ask. "You aren't military trained. How can you guys help?"

"It's kind of weird, bud, but we can." he says. "Just trust me. I wouldn't go if I didn't think it was safe. I think it is super safe. They know what they're doing, and we all feel good about it. I mean, I'll miss you like crazy, but it won't be for long. A couple of weeks. Maybe a month. I'll be home before you know it. But, you've got to get home and tell Mom and Dad that I will be fine. OK, can you do that for me?"

I just stare at him. I want to do something for him, but I don't want to lie; I don't know if I can do what he's asked. My face begins to tingle. My chest starts to pound. Paul notices.

"Hey, buddy. Calm down. Breathe for me. In, 2, 3, 4." Paul breathes like he wants me to. I start to follow his lead. An alarm blares across the schoolyard.

"Students!" a muffled voice yells through a megaphone. "Please proceed to the bus. We leave in two minutes."

Paul and I look towards the voice. A tall, blocky figure stands on the stairs of the bus. He looks directly at Paul and me. He frowns.

His look confirms what I'd already guessed: I'm not supposed to be here. His eyes shoot to the squadron that surrounds us. He flicks his head and the troops immediately understand the silent command.

Two men take hold of Paul's arms and drag him backwards.

"Paul!" I scream. Paul stumbles backwards. They won't even let him walk.

"It's OK, bud," he tries to assure me as they drag him towards the bus like a trash can being pulled to the curb.

I remember the letter. "What about the letter?" I yell. I run towards him. Two monster hands grab at me. I slip my skinny arms loose and lunge towards Paul. Paul digs a hand into his pocket. For the first time, I see fear in his face. Is he scared of his mission, or scared he won't get the letter to me?

He barely gets the letter out of his pocket as the soldiers deliver him to the bus. He tries to throw it, but his arms are bound. He opens his hand. The letter drops. I dive to the ground and crawl to the letter. A hand grabs my leg. I reach for the letter. I'm too far away. I scoop a handful of dirt with my fingers and sling it backwards.

The captor releases my leg to wipe the dirt out of his eyes and mouth. I scramble the rest of the way to the letter. I grasp it, crumble it, and shove it into my pocket.

Out of breath again, I surrender to the ground. I look at the bus stairs. Paul has vanished into the bus. The last few students climb the stairs, none of them pausing to look at me. The campus is empty, except for me and the few soldiers who resume a hawkish position over my helpless body.

The man who yelled through the megaphone parts their formation. He approaches me. He bends down to meet me on the ground. "Are you OK, son?"

Saliva fills my mouth. My nerves warm, then burn. Nausea overwhelms me. The man starts again: "Son, can you hear me? What's your name? We can get you some help." His face is bent out of focus like a computer glitch. Every color in my field of vision shifts a few colors around the color wheel. The man's face turns yellow. His green hat goes blue. The bright blue summer sky morphs into a horrific purplish-red.

Twinkling stars fill the air around my face. Each star explodes in violent succession. They crash into each other until they become a single pane of blinding light. I can't hear the explosions because of the ringing in my ears. One last unbearable flash. The rings stab the deepest part of my head.

Finally, black.

Chapter 3

I open my eyes. My bedroom light spins on the ceiling above me. Sharp pain pulses through my head. My stomach churns. I try to stay still because I know this feeling. A single move will send the contents of my stomach hurling across my room. It's all painfully familiar, the worst feeling I know: I've had a seizure.

Where was I when it happened? Did it happen at school? I hate it when it happens at school. I never know what I've said to people. I don't remember much of what I say and do right before and after seizures, but I'm never *myself*. It's like some monster overtakes my body and makes me act like a crazed lunatic for a bit.

If it happened at school, did I scream at my classmates? Did they make fun of me? I can only imagine the looks I'll get when I go back to school. If I go back.

I continue to stare at the ceiling. I need my stomach to stop blending its contents before I sit up. "Just breathe," I whisper to myself. I try not to worry about school or doctors or new medicine.

"Wait!" I say to myself. "School is out. I was at school. It was the last day of...Paul."

I sit up quickly. Too quickly. My stomach rumbles like the earth before a volcano erupts.

Here it comes. You better get to a toilet.

I leap out of bed and sprint for the bathroom. The room won't stop spinning. I stumble sideways and slam into the wall. I missed the door I had aimed for. Leaning on the wall, I slip down until I crumble on the floor. My stomach heaves.

Just keep it down. Get to the toilet.

I grip the door jam and use it as a handle. I pull myself to the bathroom and slide across the floor. I see the toilet, a few feet in front of me. Oh no.

The sight of the toilet tells my stomach to let go. No holding back. I lunge for the toilet bowl. My body revolts against itself. I can't control anything. The next thing I know, my insides float in the toilet bowl water in front me. A gooey string of spit sags from my lips and dangles towards the water. The sight of it sickens me. I heave again.

And then there's the smell: that bitter acid of stomach bile mixed with fading bathroom cleaner. The smell brings round two. Anything that was left in my stomach is now surely in the toilet. I flush the toilet and collapse to the floor.

I know this drill too well. Throwing up eases some of the pain. It always does. And now the cool bathroom floor tiles provide some relief too. In a few minutes, I'll be able to get up off the floor without stumbling sideways.

I stay sprawled out on the floor for the prescribed time. I grab the bathroom sink. I pull myself to my knees, then my feet.

I shuffle back to bed. Mom walks in.

"Oh, honey," she says in her soft, comforting voice. "Did you get sick?"

I nod.

"You had an episode at school," she says as she put her arms around me.

"I know," I reply.

I glance up at her. Her eyes look tortured. Her mascara has bled down her cheeks. She's been crying. Why? My seizures always make her sad, but this seems extreme. Something is different. What happened?

"Mom, what's wrong?"

Her eyes well up. Memories pop in my head. They're random, and out of order. Paul. Something happened to Paul. "It's Paul, right?" I ask. "What happened to Paul, Mom?"

She clasps her hands over her mouth. She tries to wall off tears and choke back cries. The pain she's holding back makes me feel sick again. My head still pounds. That awful look on her face makes it worse.

"Maggie," Dad's voice calls from downstairs. "The President's coming on. Better get down here."

Mom collects herself. She wipes the tears from her eyes. The mascara smears further across her cheeks. "Chance, you need to get more rest. Don't worry about Paul. Everything is under control. Lay back down, hon. Go to sleep. We'll tell you everything you need to know later. I need to go be with your dad for a bit, but I'll check on you after a while." She dabs a final tear from her eye, takes a deep breath, and turns for the door.

She leaves my room. I hear her footsteps descend the stairs. I close my eyes hoping it will help me drum up memories from the last few days. What happened to Paul?

"Paul," I say aloud. "What happened to you?" My mind races. It makes my head hurt worse. "No," I argue with my body. I grab my head and throw myself back onto my bed. I can't remember. I never remember. Seizures take my memory. The few glimpses of the week before a seizure always come back in jumbled bits and pieces. They're so mixed up I don't know what to trust. But this time, I need to remember. Something has happened to my brother, and it has Mom in tears.

My breath picks up. Frustration simmers. My nerves heat up. I reach into my pocket to feel for the pill. Before my hand touches it, though, I feel a piece of paper. I pull it out of my pocket. It's just a crumpled scrap, but I unfold it and find a scribbled note in Paul's handwriting:

mom and pops,
i'm fine. don't worry about me. the country needs my help,
and i know i can help. i've got puinn and jake and some

other guys with me. general palmer says we qrob won't
go to combat and we'll be home in a couqle of weeks. love
you guys. tell Chance the same.

love,
P

"The bus," I say. "He got on a bus."

Yesterday starts coming back. The upper school students: they all left. We got out of school early because of an emergency. The day races through my head like a video clip bouncing around at triple speed. I don't know what to believe. I should tell Mom and Dad. I rise to my feet, and start to rush out of the room.

It's too soon to run.

The dizziness returns. Blood rushes to my head and starts pounding in my skull. I stop. But my parents need to know. I leave my room, slowly this time. I carefully descend the stairs. As I near the bottom, I hear a news anchor's voice from the television:

"And now, we'll switch over to the President, as he is ready to address the nation."

"Americans," the President starts. "As most of you know, two years ago our nation instituted an unprecedented and mandatory registration process for all teenagers fifteen and older. This was a precautionary procedure to prepare for the potential need to enter some of our young Americans into a draft if needed to arm our military with soldiers enhanced through self-directed evolutionary techniques. We had hoped that we would never be forced to utilize this draft, and the US military and our allies have taken every step possible to keep this revolutionary technology out of the hands of bad actors. Putting such technology in the hands of the wrong people could greatly endanger our citizens and our country. No one wants the youth of this country to be turned into so-called 'super soldiers' merely because growing minds and bodies are capable of being manipulated. Unfortunately, the need for this draft has come, and one such draft has now been successfully executed."

"Yesterday, a small number of young adults between the ages of sixteen and nineteen were securely removed from one school to beta test the draft. No students were harmed, and all the students are safely in the custody of our military in a highly secured location. All students were given the opportunity to decline selection, and we are grateful for the students that bravely chose to serve their country. Thankfully, we do not currently expect any of these young adults to see active combat. Our goal is to resolve the emergency circumstances using diplomatic tactics, and if needed, traditional military methods. However, out of an abundance of caution, and because of the unique threat to our nation and the world, we have begun preparations."

"These young adults will be awarded with the highest military honor regardless of the outcome, and we are forever indebted to them for their bravery. If you are a family member of one of these young adults, we thank you for your bravery as well. Your country will do all that it can to support you. If you know one of these families, I ask that you wrap around them with love and support. These are trying times, and it's through community that we will hold each other up and build a stronger nation than ever before."

"For more details, I will hand it over to General Palmer, who is leading this operation."

Mom and Dad watch the television, motionless. I stand behind them. They don't know I'm there. I creep up to them and stand by their sides. I look at their faces, their blank faces. Where have I seen that face? Ms. Porter. Their faces look just like Ms. Porter's after she received news of the emergency.

The news anchor came back to the screen.

"Now, we see General Davis Palmer taking the podium with Dr. Genesis Jacobs following. As most of us know, Dr. Jacobs has been a leading researcher for self-directed evolution and is frequently brought into controversial discussions about the topic of the so-called 'super soldier' movement that many have feared since the concept of the draft was considered years ago. It now looks like General Palmer is ready to address the nation."

"Thank you, Mr. President. Earlier this week, a terrorist organization gained control over a joint research facility of the US and other allied nations in the northeast regions of Asia, formerly called Siberia when it was controlled by Russia. As many of you know, the area has been largely occupied under treaty by the largest coalition of nations in the history of the world to conduct highly experimental testing related to the exploration of mining other planets and alternative fuels. Based on certain intelligence, we have reason to believe that the terrorist organization who gained control of the area is using ground forces made up of advanced foot soldiers. The advanced methods of such soldiers lead us to believe that they are the realization of self-directed evolutionary techniques, or, as they have become known in the popular culture, 'super soldiers'."

"Currently, the terrorist organization is limited to an isolated region which we have been able to contain without direct altercation. The draft conducted yesterday was a precautionary measure, and we will use self- directed evolutionary techniques with the young adults now in military custody as a last result only. However, as Dr. Jacobs will explain, young adults are the primary candidates for such techniques given their biological state of development. Therefore, we have taken these brave young adults into military custody out of an abundance of caution."

"No!" Mom yells. Her knees shake. She falls to the ground. Dad drops down to hold her. "No! No! No! They can't do this. No!"

My heart races. I can feel my pulse beating in my temples, my fingers, my throat. My head feels like someone's driving an oversized nail into it. The room starts to spin like my bedroom ceiling did just a few minutes ago. I need to puke again. I dry heave a few times. There's nothing left to throw up. I fall to my knees. I dry heave again. And again.

I look back to Mom and Dad who are locked in a helpless embrace. They weep together on the den floor. I look back to the TV screen. Dr. Jacobs has started taking questions from the press. I can't hear what he's saying over my parents' crying and the ringing in my ears. I reach for the pill in my pocket. Again, the letter.

"Mom, Dad," I say.

"It's going to be alright, Chance," Dad assures me, choking back his own sobs. "We'll get him back. It will be fine."

"Here," I hold the letter out in front of me. "Paul gave it to me before he left. He said he would be OK."

Dad snatches it out of my hand. He reads it. He passes it to Mom, and buries his face in his hands. Mom reads the letter, and covers her mouth. She tries to hold back more weeping.

"P's and Q's," she says. "Oh, my boy. His P's and Q's."

I want to be strong for Paul. It feels like I *need* to be strong for Paul. I touch the pill in my pocket. "Not, yet," I think to myself. I just need some room to breathe. Breathe, and calm down. I head towards the backdoor. My treehouse waits for me in the backyard. I won't get the summer I wanted, but some form of peace waits in that treehouse. It always does.

Chapter 4

I open the door to the backyard walk towards the treehouse. My stomach is still woozy and my head swims with confusion about Paul and the President and super soldiers. I don't want to deal with all of this right now, not while the world is still somewhat spinning around me. At least I can walk in a straight line.

I try to shake it all from my mind. I need to calm down, at least until the symptoms go away, but I can't. I reach the ladder and climb up. I enter the treehouse through a hole in the floor. Despite my change in scenery, I can't stop thinking of three things: Paul is gone; my parents are a wreck; and the summer I had planned, I had waited for, isn't going to happen. At least the treehouse is here, calling me to enter and rest and breathe. But it doesn't feel restful. I should try some breathing exercises, but I can't focus. Paul, Super soldiers—I can't think of anything else.

I can't control anything, and that weighs on me. The pressure builds. Stars slowly fill the treehouse. I close my eyes, hoping they'll go away. They don't. Instead, they appear a little faster and a little brighter with each moment.

"No, not now," I tell myself. This is supposed to be my place of peace. The doctors even say so. It's here that I can escape from anything the world throws at me and focus on staying calm. I reach my hand into my pocket. The pill is still there. I don't want to take it. I don't want to miss a week of life sleeping. I can't, not right now. I need to figure out what's going on with Paul. I need to stay strong for my parents.

The thought of *staying strong* makes it worse. I don't know how to *stay strong*. It's just something people tell my parents to encourage them when I'm sick. My nerves warm up, and stars rapidly spread throughout the treehouse's interior atmosphere. If I didn't know what those stars meant, I'd welcome the pretty sight. How many treehouses come with their own star show?

"No, please no," I say.

I sit up. I feel like I might puke again. I rest my arms on one of the window ledges and sigh. A gentle breeze pats my face and brings a moment of relief. I look up through the window.

Who is that?

An unshaven man with dark stubble squats at the end of the tree branch. He wears an oversized, slouchy toboggan hat that flops on the back side of his head. The rest of his clothes are equally strange. His shirt looks like a potato sack made of a patchwork quilt. His pants stop a few inches above his ankles. He looks tidy, but from a different time or maybe a different world. His sandals are strapped to his feet in a complicated web of bands. Yes, his attire is strange, but his showing up at the end of a tree branch that shouldn't hold the weight of an adult is stranger.

While I try to process his presence and his odd appearance, the band around his right wrist catches my attention. It's wider than a watch band, but it seems to be embedded in his wrist. I've never seen the material it's made of. It's translucent and looks as if it could be filled with something; maybe a liquid or a gas. I can't take my eyes off it. As I stare, it fills with a gray, cloudy substance. Fog seems to waft around his wrist, but it's confined to within the band. I lean forward, entranced. The fog clears and is replaced by pulses of blue and green streaks that rush through the band around his wrist. I'm drawn to it. I rise to my feet and start to swing a leg out through the treehouse window.

Wait, what's going on? What am I doing? I break my trance-like stare.

I look down at my feet. I'm still mostly in the treehouse. I pull my one leg back in to safety. I glance back at the stranger. He's still there. But he's moved closer. He's within a few yards, just outside the treehouse window. I blink my eyes. This can't be real. I shake my head, hoping it will erase this image from my brain. I reopen my eyes. He's sensed my unease. He backtracks a few steps. He slowly holds his hands out in front of him, as if he's approaching a wild animal.

This guy can't be real.

You'd better get back inside, Chance. Now you've started seeing things. You can't afford to get sicker now.

Seizures have never made me hallucinate. Are things getting worse? It would make sense. The last twenty-four hours have probably been the most stressful of my life.

I reach into my pocket. I pull out the pill and look at it in my hand. I should take it. I probably *need* to take it. My world has unraveled and now my brain is doing the same. I look back out the window. He's still there. He stares at me. His face remains expressionless, his head cocked a little to the side. He seems to be sizing me up, like he wants to know what I'm made of.

"No," I say. "This can't be happening. You aren't real. Go away."

His face twinges. It's the first sign of emotion he's expressed. He braces himself for a follow up outburst. I stay silent. I try to convince myself he isn't there. He relaxes into a more comfortable position. The muscles in his face loosen. He smirks. I can't tell if it's a slight smile or a frown.

He doesn't go away. What does he want? He starts to look disappointed with me. He backs further away from the window. His casual backpedaling makes me nervous. There's a fourteen foot drop below him, and he's paying zero attention to it. His disregard strengthens my belief that he isn't real. A normal person, a *real* person, would grasp onto that branch with all their strength to avoid the fall. They'd move inches at a time to keep balance. This guy galivants in reverse down a crooked limb as if nothing can go wrong.

What is happening to me?

I move to pop the pill into my mouth. I stop, realizing that would be a bad idea. The pill will stop a seizure, but I'll be asleep in minutes. I'll be stuck out here, in the treehouse. If my parents find me knocked out here, they'll think something bad has happened. I don't need that. They don't need that.

Weighing my options makes me dizzy. I'm not sure I can make it back down the ladder. My eyes bounce back and forth from the treehouse ladder to the man who continues his relentless staring. If I start down that ladder, I'll puke at best. Fall at worst.

What should I do?

You need to get out of here.

I glance out the window, once more. I yell: "Stop, looking at me!"

"Oh, great," I say. "Now, I'm talking to him. He isn't real, but here I am talking to him. Stop talking to him."

"Just go away. I've got to get inside," I plead with him. "You aren't real, and you aren't going to make me have a seizure. Look." I hold out my hand to show him the pill, as if it is some sort of weapon against him. "I'm going down this ladder. I'm going to sleep. And when I wake up, you will not be here. You aren't real, and I never want to see you again."

I close my eyes tight and try to squeeze him out of my brain. I want him to be nothing more than a bad dream. When I open my eyes, I try to focus on the ladder and avoid looking out the window. I stumble out of the treehouse and run towards the backdoor. I reach out and grab the doorknob. Before I go in, I take one last glance backwards.

He's still there.

He puts both hands straight out in front of him, as if to say, *It's OK. I'm not going to hurt you.* His attempt to communicate makes me more nervous. I turn from him and rush inside. I slam the door behind me.

"Chance?" Mom asks, spooked by the slammed door. "What is it, honey? What's wrong?" She hurries to me. She knows I'm upset. "We are going to get Paul back. It's going to be fine."

"Mom, I think I need to take the pill," I say. I bury my head against her chest. Dad joins and wraps his arms around us both.

"I think that's a good idea, buddy," Dad says. "There's a lot going on right now, a lot of stuff we need to figure out. It's going to be fine, but it's going to be pretty stressful for a while. If you are feeling bad, take that pill and let's get you to bed. Hopefully, when you come to, we'll have everything figured out. I'll get you some water."

I stay in Mom's arms while Dad fetches the water. Tears stream down my face. Dad returns. Why am I so weak? Why can't I deal with this? Why can't I help? Paul would help me. Why can't I help him?

"Here, bud," Dad says and hands me a glass.

I push back from Mom and take the glass with one hand. I put my other hand in my pocket and grab the pill. I pull it out and hold it in my upturned palm. I stare at it, disgusted. Sure, this will ensure I don't have a seizure but it feels like I'm wimping out.

I'm a coward.

"It's OK, Chance," Mom says. "We're proud of you for making this decision."

"It takes strength to admit you need help, Chance," Dad reassures me. "Let's take the pill and get you upstairs."

I put the pill in my mouth. I take a drink of water. I swallow the water, but keep the pill hidden in my cheek.

"Good man," Dad says taking the glass again. "Now, let's get you to bed."

Neither noticed my trick. Mom and Dad follow me up the stairs and into my room. They pull back the covers for me, and I climb into bed. They cover me up.

"We'll see you in a few days, buddy," Dad says.

"I'll come check on you, and keep you fed," Mom adds soothingly. "You won't remember, but we'll make sure you get rest and your strength back. We'll have some better news about Paul when you come back to. I'm sure of it."

"OK," I say. I need them to leave now. This pill is starting to dissolve in my cheek. A chalky mess begins to coat my tongue.

"We love you, Chance," Mom says. They leave my room and close the door behind them. When I hear footsteps start down the stairs, I pull the pill out of my mouth and jump out of bed. I run to the window and look down at my treehouse. He isn't there.

Nobody's there. It was just my imagination. I sigh a huge breath of relief and look down at the wet powder the pill has left in my hand.

"Gross." At least, I don't need to take the pill. I was able to calm down on my own. That's worth something. Before I head to the bathroom to clean up, I take another peek out the window.

He's back; and he's staring straight at me. I stumble back in terror. I toss the pill mush into my mouth, force it down my dry throat, and jump into bed.

My heart races. My nerves warm up. I breathe. I count out the breaths: "in two, three, four, five, six." It's too fast. The pill isn't going to help. I try holding a big breath in. I hold it until I can't any more. A huge exhale rushes out of my lungs.

I try again: "in, two, three, four. Out, two, three, four." This time, it's slower.

Again: "in, two, three, four. Out, two, three, four." Again: "in, two, three, four. Out, two, three...."

My eyes feel heavy. My room starts to blur. My heart stops pounding. It slows. I can't feel my head. Again: "in, two...."

One week later

Chapter 5

My eyes open, but I'm not really awake. It takes determined concentration to keep my eyelids from slamming shut. I don't think I can move my arms or my legs a single inch. My body feels worthless.

I know this feeling. I must have taken the pill.

Knowing the cause of the unnatural drowsiness eases my anxiety. I know my limp body isn't the strengthless shell that it feels like. It's just recovering from some pretty strong medicine. With dogged focus, I wiggle my fingers. Then my arms. I grip the sheets with my toes and try out some other test movements. Soon I'm convinced I can sit up and get out of bed.

It will take a few days to get completely back to normal. But for now I'm calm and awake, and it's time to figure out what has happened since I took that pill.

How long have I been asleep?

I look at a clock next to my bed. It doesn't help. I don't know when I went to sleep. I roll my sandbag legs off the bed and press my feet onto the floor. I stand up, bracing against the wall for balance. I need to get myself cleaned up. I shuffle to the dresser and pull out a change of clothes. I stumble around and notice the pill bottle on my desk. I reluctantly shake out another pill and tuck it into the pocket of my jeans. The effort of all this activity leaves me fatigued, so I sit for a moment to regain my strength.

The front door slams shut, and I hear footsteps move towards the kitchen.

"Joseph," Mom calls to Dad. "We have a letter from Paul."

"Paul!" I remember. They've heard from Paul. I must get downstairs. I hear Dad's footsteps rush to meet Mom's.

"What does it say?" Dad asks. "Open it."

I try to shake the grogginess out of my body as I start down the stairs. I pause on the third or fourth step down. I preach to myself: "No episodes. Walk downstairs confidently, calmly. You aren't sick. You don't need to go back to bed."

I continue my descent. They finish reading the letter before I make it halfway. I arrive in the hallway to find my parents staring at each other. They're both equally confused.

"Did you get a letter from Paul?" I ask. "What does it say? Can I read it?"

Mom looks up at me, a shocked expression on her face. She tries to smile at me, but gives up with a sigh.

"Chance, you're up. Are you feeling okay?"

I nod and ask for the letter again. Mom hesitates, but Dad pulls the letter from her hand and thrusts it at me. I look down at the formal military letterhead. The first four words shock me:

Dear Mother and Father...

Mother and Father? What? Paul never calls Mom and Dad *Mother* and *Father*. Mom was *Mom* and Dad was *Pops*. For as long as I can remember, that's what Paul has called them, even when he wasn't supposed to.

I read on. It gets worse.

Please know that I am well and continue to grow in courage and health as we carry out Project Delta. My teammates are great. We all encourage each other as we are away from our friends and family. Obviously, we were all taken by surprise, but we're all happy to be here. It's a privilege to serve our country. It's been quite an experience seeing all of this top secret stuff. We live in an amazing country. Luckily, they don't think we'll be here much longer. The conflict seems to be coming under control. If the situation continues to improve, we should be home in a few more weeks. I miss you guys and will continue to write as I am able.

Sincerely,
Paul

"Please know that I'm well..."

"Coming under control..."

"Write as I am able..."

Paul doesn't say stuff like that. And what about the P's & Q's? They're all correct. Dad used to tell Paul that his dyslexic mix up of P's and Q's was just putting his personal touch on everything he writes. "Think of it as your signature style," he'd tell Paul.

Paul didn't write this letter. I know that for a fact, and so do Mom and Dad. I look back to their faces. Their expressions are caught between blank confusion and uncertain frustration. They don't know what to do. What are they going to do?

"Mom," I interrupt the silence. "It doesn't look like—"

"I know, Chance," she replies.

Dad storms towards the garage. He won't yell in front of me. He can't even get mad in front of me. He slams the door harder than ever before, though. If Paul's dyslexia is his signature writing, Dad's slamming the door is his signature way of saying, "I'm mad."

"It's OK, honey." Mom reaches out to hug me. She wants to comfort me, but her chest heaves as she chokes back tears. There is nothing comforting about this.

"No," I say. "It's not OK. No. I just need—" My heartbeat ticks faster. My nerves heat up.

"Chance, we're going to figure it out. Your father is frustrated, but he will calm down, and we'll make a plan."

I turn away from her and walk towards the back door. I'm not conceding to bed this time. I need to be strong for Paul and my parents now. My health cannot be a distraction. I grab the doorknob. I yank the door open. I want to slam it shut, just like Dad. But before I follow through, I think about Mom.

"I'm OK, Mom." I assure her. "I just need to calm down a bit. I'm headed to the treehouse. I'm fine. We'll figure it out, right? I'm fine. I'll be out there if you need me."

I walk out, pulling the door closed gently behind me. As if to make up for not slamming the door, I find myself clenching my jaw and stomping through the yard. I fume. I think about the look on that General's face. I saw it on the bus; I saw him on the news; I saw him in my dreams. Our whole country trusts this guy, but I don't. And I can't do anything about it.

You better calm down. Otherwise, you'll be headed back to bed with another pill.

"Shut up!" I whisper-scream at myself. I climb the ladder slowly and make my way to the treehouse floor. I sit down. I breathe: *in, two, three, four. Out, two, three, four.* I try to ignore my pocket and what's inside it. I will calm myself down on my own. I don't need any help.

It takes a few minutes, but I get myself under control. I look out the window.

He's there again.

I shove myself backwards across the treehouse floor. My back slams into the wall, stopping my retreat.

"Strange, no?" he asks.

Oh, no. He's talking now. I jam my hand in my pocket. The pill is there waiting for me. I can scarf it down and escape this moment. But again, I don't want to.

"You," I hiss. "Who are you? No, wait. You aren't real." I pause for a few seconds to catch my breath. I look away from him and scratch my forehead. I look back up. He's still there. The two of us stare at each other. "What do you mean, 'strange'?" I ask.

"The letter," he replies.

"See, you aren't real," I say. "You are in my mind. That's the only way you could know what the letter says."

"I won't try to prove to you that I'm real, Chance. You are free to ignore reality to your own destruction."

"OK, then go away, please," I say.

"Fair enough." He turns his shoulder as if starting to walk away. "Are you sure?" He asks.

"Well, hold on," I say. "Just, tell me. Are you real?" "More real than anything you've ever seen," he says.

"What?"

"Chance, I'll be brief. I don't waste time on fools who despise instruction. Likewise, I'm not here to scare you. I will instill what's needed. I'm here to help you."

"Help me?" I ask. "With what? It's my brother who needs help."

"Ah, yes. I'm aware of your brother and his circumstances. But, contrary to what you might think, it's you, Chance, who can help him. Yes, it's you who can help him, and me who can assist you."

"What?" I ask again. This guy is confusing. Why am I even talking to him? I'm not convinced he's real, and his explanations aren't helping. "What do you mean, *help me*? Do you mean, cure me of the episodes?"

"Is that what they call it: *episodes*?" He mumbles some frustration under his breath.

"Yes," I say. "I have a disability."

"Ah," he grumbles. The noise is sort of a half laugh, half scoff. "You call it a *disability*. I call it *access*. Those episodes. They are energy. They are power. It's your gift, the gift that will allow you to be who you were meant to be. But, as long as you see it as a weakness, you'll never taste any of its potential."

"OK, you've got to tell me what on earth you are talking about," I say. I rise to my feet and try to sound stern. He's making me mad with this nonsense. I want him to know I'm serious. There's no way my seizures are actually a *power*. If he's going to help me, he needs to be clear.

"Ah, yes. There's a spark of spirit." He swings a leg in the treehouse window and enters. He interpreted my attempt to intimidate him as an invitation to come closer.

"Be straight with me, now," I say. "Please." I hold up a hand to stop him. "Who are you? What are you doing here? And how are you going to help me?" I look at him. I wish for bravery in my eyes, but I'm sure they show fear. He smiles. Before he answers,

I add: "And tell me again, how are you real?"

He sighs. He turns his head to the side and pinches the bridge of his nose. He mumbles to himself and gently shakes his head. He returns his eyes to me. "If I must. You may call me Esri. I'm unlike you, a human that is. I'm an Omnituen. I come to help you realize that those *episodes*, as you call them, are not something that you need cured. No, rather, they are a unique power. You were created to harness it, and you may be able to use it to benefit the world. And not just the world you will live in for some amount of time before you die, but also the world I will live in for generation after generation through a dimension that very few humans will ever realize exists. You, Chance, are already one of the few who knows this dimension exists, because you see me now. Others cannot.

I was confused before. But now I'm as confused as I've ever been. Pre-algebra confused. He approaches me. The band around his wrist glows.

"Regarding *realness*, as you say, I propose a question back to you. I was created ten thousand years ago; and you, you'll be lucky to live for one hundred years. So, who seems more real, you or me?"

I shake my head. My mind overflows with confusion and disbelief. I had hoped his answering my questions would clear things up, but it's only confused things more. I want to ask more questions, but he abruptly cuts me off with a swift hand outstretched before him.

"For now, that concludes any and all explanation. To proceed, I need a commitment from you."

"A commitment to do what?"

"You want your brother back, correct?"

"Yes, of course."

"You will do anything to get him back, correct?"

"Well, yeah."

"Anything?" he repeats.

"I said, *Yes*. Without question." My resolve grows, "What else do you want from me? What does this have to do with commitment?" I ask. My face feels hot.

"Ah, yes." He pauses. His eyes narrow and he seems to read my face. "If saving your brother means more *episodes,* as you say, and throwing that little pill away, will you still commit to do *anything*?"

I hesitate to answer. I pat the outside of my pocket. It's there. I take a long, deep breath. "I… I guess," I say.

"Not enough; lukewarm," he rebukes. He turns and starts towards the window where he had entered. He lifts one foot onto the sill. He's leaving.

"Wait!" I yell. "Yes. I'll—".

He turns back and marches towards me. He looks me dead in the eyes. His gaze digs into my eyes like he's searching for something hidden.

"Anything?" he questions.

"Anything," I affirm.

He holds up his right arm and makes a fist, stretching it out like he wants a fist bump. The band around his wrist starts to glow. Wild colors appear and then transform over and over. It looks like the colors that appear when I close my eyes and massage the outside of my eyelids. The greens morph to blues, then reds, then yellows, and oranges. It's like a rainbow that doesn't know how to organize its stripes. My eyes fix on the band until Esri commands my attention.

"Look at me, Chance," he says. "If you commit, press your fist upon mine."

I raise my arm, the arm that I could barely move less than an hour ago. Our fists touch, and for the first time, I feel how the entire world is spinning. The treehouse, the summer sky above it, and the grassy yard below it all rush around my head. I've become the axis upon which the world rotates. I try to catch up, like I often try to follow individual fan blades as they rotate on the ceiling above my bed. But this is too fast. I've committed to something. I don't know what. But I know everything has changed. Changed forever. For some reason I know that things will never go back to *normal*.

As the spinning becomes too much to bear, most of the world around me begins to fade away. Soon only the treehouse remains. Outside there is only empty space.. Within the treehouse walls, the stars that frequently show up before a seizure swarm my field of vision. Unlike the usual chaotic glimmering, however, they organize into twinkling rows and then rush from the floor of the treehouse through the ceiling. My nerves warm to hot and the temperature continues to increase. From head to toe, energy rushes through my body. I feel like a rocket. Vitality builds within my legs, my chest, my head. I'm ready to blast off and enter another realm. My mouth waters, but I don't throw up. I look down at my fist. It's pressed against Esri's with a magnetism I couldn't break if I tried. All the pre-seizure symptoms hammer my body, but they're somehow more controlled than usual. There's an order to the typical chaos.

Esri continues his stare into my eyes. He's searching for something again. His head slightly shifts from side to side as he explores the depths of my vision. What is he looking at? My eyes? My brain? My soul? What is he looking for?

My head is starting to hurt, but then he breaks his fist from mine. "OK," he says. With this single word and the sudden separation, I involuntarily collapse to the treehouse floor. All that had spun into nonexistence comes rushing back. The treehouse is back in it's tree above the yard below the blue sky. I hear birds and can taste the thick humid air.

"It is time," he says.

My head pounds, just like it does after a seizure. "Time for what?" I ask. I lift myself onto my knees. I have to stop moving so I don't throw up. Oh, no. I dry heave once, and then hold it in so I can hear Esri's words. He's already proven himself impatient. I don't want to frustrate him now.

"Yes. It is time," he repeats, ignoring my request for an explanation. "I assume you feel sick?"

"No, I'm heaving on the ground because I feel wonderful," I snark.

"Ah. Sarcasm. Good," he replies. "You are doing better than I expected. Go. Get somewhere to rest. Your energy is depleted. When you awake, you should feel relief. I'll return, and we will begin."

"I still don't know what you mean," I say. "Begin what?"

"You said *anything*, Chance," he says. He turns and walks towards the window.

"I know, but it would be helpful to know what I'm getting into," I say. Another dry heave interrupts. I take a deep breath, exhale, then swallow. "So I can prepare myself."

"I've told you how to prepare. Get rest. Rid yourself of that headache. You're no good in this state."

"That's it?" I ask. "Get some sleep?"

"Nothing you've seen or even imagined will prepare you for the journey we're about to take together. You will soon find out who you really are and what you were created for. The best advice I can offer is to be rested. Understood?"

"Fine," I concede. Then he's gone. I presume he went out through the window, but I can't be sure. One moment he's there, and the next, nothing.

Chapter 6

My face rests uncomfortably on a hard wooden surface. My mouth is dry. I smack my lips a few times to try to draw up some saliva and feel gritty particles caught in my teeth. I open my eyes. I'm on the treehouse floor. I must have fallen asleep soon after Esri left. I sit up and look out the window. The sun edges lower in the sky, but it's not evening yet. I feel rested, but my head aches.

"What did that guy do to me?" I ask myself. I now know he's real. But can I trust him?

I pat my pocket. The pill rests in its usual spot. Good, just in case. What did he call himself? An *Omni-what?* I look out at the tree branch, then out the other window. I survey the entire backyard. He's gone for now.

I should go back to the house. Has Dad come back yet? Has he calmed down? What about Mom? Hopefully their days have been more restful than mine. I wonder if any more newscasts have played, or if they've been in touch with anyone with information.

I climb down the treehouse ladder and head towards the backdoor.

Before walking in the house, I turn and check the treehouse and surrounding branches one last time. No sign of Esri. He's gone. It's time to go back in and face reality.

I walk in. I hear Mom and Dad talking at the kitchen table. They lower their voices when they hear the door shut. They don't want to stress me out with everything they're dealing with. But, honestly, they're terrible at hiding it. Besides, I'm dealing with it too. Why do they still hide these kinds of things from me?

I enter the kitchen and try to sound cheerful. "Hey" I say.

"Hey, bud," Dad says. "Listen, sorry about storming out earlier. I wasn't mad at you or at Mom, or Paul, or any of us. I was mad at the situation. I'm worried about Paul, obviously, and want more details. I can't control it, and that made me mad. But I shouldn't have acted that way. I'm sorry.

"It's OK," I say. "Any more news?"

"No, nothing yet," Dad replies. "But we're going to figure it out. I've made a couple of phone calls, and if we don't hear something soon, I'll head out on my own. I'll find him."

"OK," I say. If Esri was right and it's going to take some so-called *power* of mine to find Paul, it seems like Dad going after Paul on his own won't help the situation. I don't know who to believe, but none of the present options seem great. I pat my pocket. It's there. I'm safe.

"Well, I hope we hear something soon then," I say. "It would be nice to keep the rest of us together until Paul comes back. You know?" I try to gently dissuade Dad from going after Paul, just in case Esri is right.

"We know, honey," Mom says. "We agree, and that's the hope."

"OK," I say. "I'm going to head upstairs for a while. I'll probably go to bed early tonight. I'm still pretty tired from the pill, you know?"

"Good idea, bud," Dad assures me.

I walk upstairs and jump onto my bed. I don't know what to think. Will we hear anything from the government? Is Dad going to go after Paul? Who should I trust? What should I do? I can already tell my thoughts are on overdrive. That means a sleepless night. Not good for an epileptic. I prepare myself for hours of breathing exercises and palm rubbing.

However, before I know it, my eyes creak open. The sun is rising. I had fallen asleep in my clothes while thinking about Paul and Esri and slept clear through the night. I know what Mom's reaction will be: "Your body must have needed it."

I bounce myself out of bed and walk downstairs. My head feels pretty clear; better than it has in days, maybe even months. I don't know what my role in getting Paul back will be, but I'm ready to help. I feel calm, ready to play my part.

I enter the kitchen where I had left my parents the night before. They don't look up this time. They both stare at a computer screen, fully engaged in something.

"It says, click on this link and use your social security number to start the process," Dad says to Mom, their eyes not leaving the screen.

"Hey," I say.

"Oh, hey, hon," Mom says. "There was another announcement on the news this morning. They said that the parents of the kids affected would be contacted and invited to speak to General Palmer and Dr. Jacobs. They are going to clear up some of the misunderstanding and tell us when we'll get Paul back. Dad's just trying to log on now. As you can imagine, the security is pretty tight."

"That's great," I say. "When is the call?"

"We're logging on now," Mom says hesitantly. "Chance, we don't think it's a good idea for you to listen in. If they end up giving us bad news, we'd rather tell you ourselves than have you hear it from the General and scientist. They just...Well, they might not be the most *sensitive*, I guess."

My temples burn. This *must* be my way to help. I just know it. But they aren't going to let me. I need to know what's going on. How can I help if I don't know what's going on. I rub my thumbs against my palms, and clench my teeth together. I need to get a grip.

I silently preach to myself: "Just stay calm, and you can listen in from the other room. They'll never know you are there. If you lose it now, you'll be sent to your room with a pill jammed down your throat."

"OK, I get it," I reply as calmly as possible.

"OK, good," Mom says as she puts her palm to my cheek.

"Got it!" Dad exclaims. "We're in." He reads the message on the screen out loud: "*Your conference has not yet started. You will be automatically connected when the chairperson starts the conference.* Well, we'll wait and see what happens. Chance, why don't you step out, and we'll catch you up just as soon as we finish. Sound good?"

"Yeah, OK," I say.

I walk to the staircase. I stomp my feet on a few stairs to make it sound like I'm going up to my room. I pause until I hear Mom and Dad start talking freely. I hear their voices rise to a normal level, and I tiptoe back towards the kitchen. I make my way to the wall just outside the entryway. I slide silently down the wall and sit cross- legged. I, like my parents, wait for the conference to begin.

"Babe, the conference is starting now," Dad says to Mom. I can hear her as she runs water at the kitchen sink, probably filling some glasses.

"OK, coming," Mom says.

Their chairs squeak as they settle in for the conversation. I hear them shift in their seats. They're nervous. I'm nervous. But I can't bounce, or pick, or move at all. I can't let them know I'm here.

Silence fills the air as we wait for the General to speak. The soundlessness floods the entire house with uncertainty. I feel it. I smell it. Finally, the sound of a strong man clearing his throat pops the soundless bubble.

"Good morning," General Palmer starts. "Thank you for joining. We appreciate your interrupting your days to join this call. We apologize for the short notice. We only decided to host this call after hearing many concerns about the project. Specifically, the lack of communication and the potentially confusing messaging. First and foremost, I want to apologize for this shortcoming. As the project lead, that's on me. We've obviously never conducted a project of this nature, and we thought a certain communication plan would be best received by the families, and it turned out that plan was wrong. That brings me to the first issue I want to address: the letter the families received from the project participants—er—your children. That letter was not written by your child, as most of you have probably already figured out. We thought that a letter that had your child's name on it would help put you at ease. However, we did not anticipate that you all would be concerned by the fact that it wasn't your child writing the letter and that would cause more confusion and greater distrust. For that, I am sorry. It was a bad decision.

"Secondly, an update on the participants, your children. They're all doing well and progressing nicely. I must say, I was blown away by their willingness to volunteer, and that has translated to high levels of engagement with all of the early exercises and assessments. They are bonding with each other, and I continue to hear again and again about their common sense of *mission* and *service*. It's truly remarkable. You should all be very proud of your children. You have clearly done a wonderful job raising them, and they are demonstrating noble service as I'm sure you would all expect.

"Now, as you see, Dr. Jacobs has joined me, and he is here to answer any of the, the ah, the science-based questions. I will take any questions regarding the project in general and its purpose. Now, there are quite a few families on this web call, so we can't just let you start blurting out questions. You will see that there is a chatbox in the lower right hand portion of the screen. If you will write five questions in that box, we will collect them and start to answer. Our assumption is that many of you will have the same questions, so we will take the next five minutes to let you type your questions, and we will take another five to consolidate the questions so we are addressing topics most important to you as families. So, Dr. Jacobs and I will take a break here, and we'll see you again in ten minutes."

I lean into the wall. My shoulders loosen. My jaw relaxes. It's the best news I've heard since this nightmare began. Maybe Paul is fine. This whole *project* is just new for the military, and they don't know how to tell people about it. Now that they're talking directly to the families, it all seems more understandable. I close my eyes. I take some great big healing breaths. I breathe deeply until I hear General Palmer and Dr. Jacobs retaking their seats in the video.

"Welcome, back. Again, thank you for your time, and thank you for these questions. For the sake of expediency, I'll jump right in. First, *can you talk to your children?* Unfortunately, no, we can't allow that. It could potentially compromise the project. I'll let Dr. Jacobs elaborate."

Clumsy static replaces voices. Dr. Jacobs must have fumbled his microphone. His voice is feeble and squeaky when he comes on: "If you recall from the original registration process, the reason young adults nearing the end of adolescence make the ideal candidates for self- directed evolution therapy is the combination of their almost developed brains and bodies paired with their pliability. That goes for their brains, bones, muscles, everything. Any added stress, anxiety, or inflammation can greatly reduce this pliability. Accordingly, we need to keep the environment as controlled as possible. Allowing participants to reach out to friends or family could potentially cause stress, either good stress being excited to talk to you, or bad stress in the event that they get homesick. Either way, we cannot take the chance as it would delay successful project completion."

"Thank you, Dr. Jacobs," the General jumps in. "Next question: *will your children be sent to combat?* Good question, and the short answer is we have no current reason to believe that your children will see active combat. At the moment, we don't believe they will ever leave the United States. The situation in the conflict territory is currently contained, and we feel confident in resolving the matter using diplomatic methods and more historical military strategies, if needed. So, for now, *no,* your children won't be sent to the battlefield.

"There are a lot of questions about what is actually happening to your children," the General continued. "Will they be turned into *super soldiers*? Will they be different people? Are they being harmed? These are valid questions, and Dr. Jacobs and I will try to talk a little back and forth to explain exactly what's going on, and what you can expect to see when your children return home."

The two continue for another ten or fifteen minutes. They describe a series of procedures that Paul will go through. First, they will fine tune his immune system like a precision race car. Next, they will debug his DNA so that any slight mutations or defects will be corrected so his body can operate at maximum capacity. Then, they will reinforce his bones and muscles with chemical compounds that make them stronger, more resilient, and more powerful than other humans. Finally, his brain will be *unlocked,* as Dr. Jacobs puts it. I've always learned in science class that humans only use 10% of their brains. Dr. Jacobs uses a similar number. He explains that a series of treatments will allow Paul to utilize his entire brain.

General Palmer askes Dr. Jacobs if all of these changes will make their children different people. Dr. Jacobs rejects that idea and instead says, "Not at all. They will be better versions of themselves. Their parents will get to see them as they were born to be."

I think back to Esri's words to me: *You will soon find out who you really are and what you were created for.*

Who was Paul *born to be*? What was I *created for*? We'll find out soon.

Chapter 7

A few days pass. A fragile calm returns to our house. Mom and Dad believe General Palmer and Dr. Jacobs. The conversation between them comforted my parents.

"They are taking good care of Paul," they tell me.

I'm not so sure.

"The General basically promised us that Paul wouldn't go to active combat," Mom assures me. I know General Palmer didn't say that, but she doesn't know I was listening in.

I don't want them worrying about me, so I play along. "That's great news," I tell my parents. "Do we have any idea when he'll be back?"

They share more partially accurate sound bites from the web conference. I don't know if they exaggerate General Palmer's assurances to convince me that Paul is OK, or if they do it to convince themselves. Either way, their hopefulness seems forced and hollow. It's plain to see that any bad news will push this household on edge over a cliff with an unknown bottom. I don't know how we'll survive that fall.

Dad encourages Mom and me: "We're one day closer to getting our boy back, right?"

Mom replies as if perfectly rehearsed: "That's right. Any day now."

I'm not so sure.

Each attempt to improve the mood falls short. And the next attempt, a little shorter still. Do they believe the General? The President? Maybe they don't believe these men, but it seems like their best option. I want to ask if this is the case. I start to ask like I've started many times recently, but I stop. I stop myself each time. I don't want to mess up the peace, even if it's based on a faked and forced reality.

Maybe General Palmer and Dr. Jacobs are *my parents'* best option. But is it *the* best option? I have more options than they do. They don't know about Esri. If he is real and his words are true, they will never have him as an option. That access is mine. It's somehow tied to my disability, or power, or access, or whatever it is that I have. This thing that I've spent every moment of my life trying to keep under control now has the potential to rescue my brother. But I must stop trying to push it down; instead, I'll have to unleash it.

I'm not so sure.

How am I supposed to throw away the years of work my family has put into helping me get well? It's easy for me to drop the breathing exercises and the palm rubbing, and to ignore the trusty pill that loyally waits in my pocket.

But, what about Mom and Dad? My parents who've stayed up with me through sleepless hospital nights? And what about Paul? How many games has he played without family watching because of me? What about all the planning that goes into keeping my stress at bay and keeping me calm? And what about the mountains of medical bills? Did Esri really want me to ignore all of that just to get some new perspective on the world?

I'm not so sure.

I avoid the treehouse for days. Part of me wants to go back. But the other part can't disregard all the time, money, and effort my family puts into keeping me healthy. It would be...wrong.

Dinner comes. I've done little but pace around the house and argue with myself about Esri and his existence. Dinner is painful. From the outside, we look like a smiling family of three enjoying each other's company. Inside, however, the false pleasantries grate on my nerves. I can't take this much longer. I'd welcome an uncontrolled outburst from someone just to see something genuine. Why can't we just tell the truth?

Dad recites his new catchphrase one more time: "We're one dinner closer to getting our boy back, right?"

Now, I'm sure. I'm sure he's wrong.

"I'm full," I interrupt. " Guess I wasn't very hungry. I'm going to go to the treehouse for a bit."

"No problem, honey," Mom says. "Have some fun."

I exit the back door and pull in some breaths, deeper than any

I have felt in days. The dishonesty that pollutes the house has been making it difficult to breathe in there. Just getting outdoors brings instant relief. I stand with my back to the door until a better breathing pattern establishes. I lift my eyes to the treehouse and its surrounding branches.

There he is, standing on the branch with his arms crossed in front of his chest.

I turn my head quickly to see if my parents are watching through the window.

"Fear not," Esri says. "They can't see me. Right?"

I look at my parents for a while longer, just in case they take a glimpse into the backyard. They don't. Their expressionless faces carry on some meaningless chatter. They look like robots. I'm glad to be out of there. I head towards the treehouse. I don't even care if Esri is real. If nothing else, he'll provide an alternative to the tension in the house.

I climb the ladder. Esri is inside the treehouse when I arrive.

His eyes lock onto mine. "Be honest," he says. It's a cold welcome.

"What?" I ask. "Be honest about what?"

He grimaces. "You know what I mean. Nevertheless, I'll explain to avoid delay," he says impatiently. "You've avoided the treehouse, the Unseen, your potential...For a few days now, no? Something's kept you away. However, you aren't convinced your parents know the truth? You aren't convinced of the General or the doctor or any of it? No? You're here because you're ready to confess that, right? Alas, here we are. A few days wasted, and each day is another that puts your brother and the others at heightened risk. But, that's another story. So, please, some honesty please, Chance."

He stops. His eyes narrow, still locked on mine, begging an answer. I'm not used to him babbling this way.

"Chance?" he questions.

"I mean—Yeah, I guess," I say. Yes, he is right. But, I don't want him to know how right he is.

"Many thanks," he replies. "Thank you for letting me be honest *for* you. Now, shall we get started?"

"Wait a second," I say. Sure, he knows what's going on, but I need some answers too. Before I left my house, I wasn't convinced Esri was real. I had prepared myself to defend the calm of the house and all the sacrifices my family had made to get me better. I need something more than a little mind reading. If he's nothing but a figure my mind has created, mind reading isn't so impressive.

He sighs heavily, "What now?" He pinches his eyebrows between his forefinger and thumb. "Do tell. What is Chance's concern of the moment?"

"You say I have this power," I start. "And you are going to help me use it. Not only is it going to help me get Paul back safely, but it's going to help me become who I *was created to be* as you say. Am I just supposed to believe that and do whatever you tell me to do?"

"Yes," he confirms without hesitation.

"How? What is this *power* and this *place* where you're going to take me? And how does it help me get Paul back?"

He hesitates. He looks away, but he can't hide his frustration. He doesn't respond immediately. I can read his face when he glances back at me: *Why am I wasting my time with this kid? Is this really worth it?* After a few moments, he breaks his silence: "Fair question."

"This world you see around you—your house, your parents, your school, this treehouse. Everything you see, feel, taste, hear, and smell." He breaks his list, and thinks about what to say next. "It's not all there is, Chance. There's more to it, infinitely more. So much of what is seen around you is at the mercy of all that cannot be seen. Most humans aren't afforded the opportunity to experience this dimension of reality. We'll call the world around you the *Seen*, shall we? And then we'll call the other dimension that I'm describing the *Unseen*. The Seen is finite. You know that. You learn about it in school. The Earth is round. It's warmed by the sun and cooled by rotation and revolution. Certain elements come together and divide and work in unity so that life on Earth can continue. But it's all...limited. It's fragile. Those who work it, humans, are also limited. Limited by time, resources, and ability. You only have a certain number of years to make your mark on this world, positive or negative. This added pressure of time in human life has pushed some on to greatness and others into evil. And then those physical limitations make the Seen easy to break, even though that seems like a longshot to you. You follow?"

"Yeah, you've just described life on Earth," I reply. "That's pretty basic."

"The Earth and maybe space and some other things, but all things *Seen*," he says.

"OK, fine. The *Seen*. What about this *Unseen*?"

"Yes, it's the Unseen where I was created and where I work and where some select humans can also go." He steps towards me. "And you, Chance, are one of those."

"OK, three questions," I stop him. "What is this Unseen like? What does it have to do with the Seen? And what do my episodes have to do with it?"

"You started to get a sense of it the other day. You felt an episode coming on, but it felt more controlled, right?"

"Yes."

"Indeed. That's because you were finally directing that energy with purpose instead of without direction. Has your doctor explained to you what a seizure is?"

"Yes," I say.

"Good. You know that it starts with an electric firing in your brain that doesn't have a corresponding purpose in your body. So the firing spreads across your brain and you go into convulsions. It's simply because your body wasn't designed to use that level of brain activity. Instead, that energy was meant to transfer you from the Seen to the Unseen. But you didn't know that. And the doctors still don't know that. That's why they give you medicine to reduce that firing. They are protecting your body from your power. But it's that power that could release you into a new dimension where you can be who you were meant to be."

"OK, so this firing, if better directed, can get me to the Unseen. Fine, what good is it?"

"As I said, the Unseen is limitless. It's bounded only by thoughts and imagination. Thoughts become reality in the Unseen. Indeed, thoughts are reality. For many, this is exciting. For all, it is dangerous. Just as in the Seen, the Unseen is riddled by...evil."

"OK, so if I end up in the Unseen, how can I help Paul who is stuck here in the Seen?" I ask.

"Do you have dreams, Chance?"

"Yes, of course," I say.

"Do some of those dreams scare you?"

"Yes, nightmares."

"And some make you laugh, no?"

"Sure," I say.

"Do dreams ever compel you to action once awake, Chance?"

"Yes," I admit.

"Ah, yes then. Would you say that dreams, although you can't touch them, feel them, hear them, see them, or taste them, impact the Seen world around you then?"

"I guess," I say.

"Precisely," he says. His eyes smiled at me. He's convinced I understand what he is getting at. He thinks I understand him much more than I actually do.

"So, it's just some dreamland?" I ask. "How is running through dreamland going to help Paul come home?"

"Dreams, Chance... they're but the beginning. A mere example. In the Unseen, you will navigate reality through thoughts. You can go to Paul in thought. You can guide him. You can rescue him."

"But, they're just thoughts!" I shout. "Paul is physically gone. He is physically separated from us. And if he goes to war, he'll be in physical danger. Wishful thinking doesn't do me any good!"

He leans away from me. His hand comes to his mouth. He strokes his lower lip with his thumb.

"You don't see it," he says, like some kind of admission of guilt. "None of you get it," he says. He turns away and starts to pace around the treehouse. I've made him mad, but it doesn't make any sense to me.

"So worried about the physical, the Earth," he continues. It doesn't seem like he's talking to me, but I look around and don't see anybody else. "I should know better by now. Humans and your silly quips: *sticks and stones may break my bones.* As if bones breaking were the most serious threat."

He turns back to me and sees that I'm still with him. "The ending," he says. "That's what you humans get wrong. The saying should go: sticks and stones may break my bones, but words cut wounds so deep that they never heal, and it's thoughts and thoughts alone that decide to break bones and spit vicious words."

We stare at each other. I actually start to understand. I'm scared. It's my thoughts that lead me into pits of stress. And it's thoughts that Dr. Watt trains me to control to prevent seizures. The breathing exercises. The palm rubbing. It's all mind games to calm me down. The pill. It's just an escape from thoughts. Esri is asking me to jump to a thought-only world and do battle there.

"Ah," he says. "You see it. I can see that. Or, I guess I should say, you know it. That much, I know."

"Why can't you do it?" I ask. "You already know the Unseen. Why can't you go travel it and check on Paul and bring him back if he is in danger?"

"Because I'm not you, Chance. I'm not human. I'm an Omnituen. I was created in the Unseen for the Unseen. I communicate only with those that can access the Unseen. Your brother, your father, your mother, most everybody you know will never know I exist. I have no way of reaching them. Human to human connection through the Seen and Unseen is required. I'm here to guide you, but I can't do it for you. It's confusing now, but the unknown is always confusing. Your purpose will never be clear unless you are willing to take a step into the unknown." He pauses for a moment. His lips twitch. A question begs to come out. "Are you willing to take a step?"

I stare at him. I pat my pocket. His eyes catch my hand. He shakes his head to persuade me against it.

"Ready?" he asks.

I move my hand away from my pocket. "I guess. Let's go."

Chapter 8

Esri holds out a fist toward me. The band around his wrist lights up as it did last time. Colors swirl and streak through it. My stomach prepares for what's coming next. It lurches. I take a deep breath and brace myself for warming nerves and popping stars.

I'm nervous, but not *seizure nervous.*

"Ready?" Esri asks.

Do I really have a choice?

I lift my arm and press my fist against his. My temples warm. My field of vision widens and my focus sharpens. Stars float up from the treehouse floor and continue through the ceiling. The world around me, the Seen, I suppose, starts losing color. The treehouse walls turn gray. The support tree blackens. Some unknown force sucks the pigment from all the surfaces that surround me—floorboards, plywood walls, tree bark. Every object in sight loses its shape except for a white outline that traces the edges. If it weren't for those outlines, it would appear that I'm floating in empty space.

The air, which is ordinarily colorless, starts to swarm with waves of colors that I have never before seen or imagined. The colors waft gently in front of me, around me, and then they somehow pierce right through me. My nerves have started to cool without me realizing. My whole body starts to go numb.

Abruptly, physical sensations stop altogether; I feel nothing.

"Breathe," Esri directs. "We're almost there."

I'm actually excited to see what comes next. A blink. That's what comes next. In that blink, that fraction of a second, everything changes. The lights, the impossible colors, and the hazy outlines all vanish. They're replaced with deep, dark, nothingness.

Everything is gone. The treehouse is gone. The tree is gone. My house is gone. The Seen is gone. It feels like I've been dropped off blindfolded in the middle of a pitch black forest. The blindfold is off now. I have no idea where I am. I don't know where to go. I don't know *how* to go anywhere. There's only endless black. I could be at the bottom of the ocean or floating through space.

Esri is gone too. I look around for him. Everywhere I look, black. I look down at my feet. Black. Am I floating? What am I standing on? Am I falling? It doesn't feel like I'm falling, but what am I standing on? Maybe my eyes are closed? I force a few exaggerated blinks in hopes to focus them on something. I open my eyes wide. Still nothing. I take a step forward. Green wavy lines pulse away from my foot like water rippling away from a pebble thrown in a lake. The green ripples lose intensity as they distance themselves from my foot. Eventually, each ripple vanishes into black. I take another step, then another. The process repeats. What am I standing on?

"Nothing," I hear Esri's voice say. I look for him, but I'm not sure where to look. His voice doesn't come from any particular direction. It just exists. I have no bearings. I don't like this.

"What?" I ask. "Where are you?"

"Breathe, Chance," he says. "There is no *where* to be. Our minds are here, connected. But our minds aren't just here. They are throughout the *Unseen*. You'll experience what you think, and you'll travel to the thoughts that come to you. Take your time. Breathe. You've left a tiny, finite reality and entered a boundless world of thought. It will overwhelm you at moments, but I am with you. Just breathe."

You should panic. This isn't right.

I want to panic, but I have no physical sensations. I'm not warm. My stomach doesn't hurt.

You are stressed. You must get out of here. This isn't right. Your mind will trap you here. You need a pill.

"Esri, what's going on?" I ask. "Why can't I feel anything?"

"Breathe, Chance," he says. "Your mind has come with you, but it isn't used to a lack of senses. It wants you to fear this unknown place. Your mind, which is accustomed to the Seen, wants to warn your body through your senses. It wants your heart to race, your head to pound, your stomach to rumble. It wants your breathing to increase. It wants adrenaline to pump through your body, but there is no body to pump it through. Your mind is panicking because it's lost access to all the infrastructure it generally uses to call you to action. None of that is here in the Unseen. Just breathe, Chance."

I close my eyes. I try my breathing exercises: "In, two, three, four. Out, two, three. Wait! How am I breathing? And how have I closed my eyes if they don't exist?"

"You aren't, and you haven't," Esri replies. "But, it's OK, Chance. Just keep doing it. Your mind can make it happen. Just breathe. Keep your eyes closed until you sense safety. I'm here, and you are OK."

I continue. *In, two, three, four. Out, two, three, four.* I calm down. I open my eyes. Esri stands in front of me.

"Welcome to the Unseen." He smirks.

I look down at my feet. Rippling green lines surround them both. I lift my hands to look at them. I see nothing at first. Then I witness the opposite effect of what happened in the treehouse. My hands appear first as black shapes outlined in white. Slowly, skin-colored pigment fills in the shape of my hands. The process continues up my arms, down my torso, and through my legs. Seeing myself, or some thought of myself, standing there calms me. But am I standing here?

No, you aren't here. Get out of here.

"Don't listen to that, Chance," Esri interrupts my thoughts. "If it helps you feel comfortable to think that your body from the Seen is here in the Unseen, then accept it. Let it be...known."

"OK, then," I say. "Here I am. I am here. In the Unseen. With you, Esri, an Omnituen—a creature of and for the Unseen. Man, that's weird."

Esri chuckles, and smiles. "Ah, good. If you can joke, you are getting comfortable. Mark that comfort in your mind, because plenty of discomfort awaits you. For starters, you must rid your present mind of the mind you brought with you from the Seen."

"What? I have multiple minds?"

"Why not?" Esri asks. "Remember, there's nothing limiting you anymore. It will take practice, but step one will be to abandon all that you brought with you from the Seen. That must die for you to truly live here in the Unseen."

"What? I have to die? Then what's going to happen to my body in the Seen?"

"It will be where you left it," Esri tries to assure me. "Excuse my word choice. It was, perhaps, a bit strong for the moment"

"Geez. It's too weird talking about my body as an *it*, like it's not mine. Or one of my minds trying to forget the other one. If I had a body right now, I'm sure it would have a headache."

Esri moves closer to me, and stares into my eyes. He isn't laughing. He has that *searching* face again. "Yes, Chance. That's it. You're already able to recognize that your body here is a creation of your mind. That's important. It will help you travel the Unseen more quickly. All that is visible, or heard, or felt, or tasted here... it's done by thought alone. The infinite nature of the Unseen is both the source of its true power and its inherent limitation. Recognizing the power of thought to operate in this world is essential to being effective."

"OK, I guess." I try to keep up. "Shall we explore a bit?"

"Let's," I say sarcastically, as if I have any idea how to explore this thought-world.

"What's something you've always wanted to try, but haven't ever been able to?" Esri asks.

"Riding a motorcycle."

"Good," Esri replies. "What kind?"

"I don't know. I don't really know anything about motorcycles. I guess something fast and aerodynamic."

"Ah, good. Go on," Esri says. "What color?"

I answer *black*. I describe what I imagine to be the perfect motorcycle: flawlessly aerodynamic for mind blowing speed and embellished with chrome detailing to contrast the smooth, dark paint job. As I describe the bike, an object appears in the distance. Each new detail brings more clarity to the object. It's clearly a motorcycle. It's my motorcycle, the one I just put into words. Actually, no, my words weren't clear enough to describe what is in front of me. Instead, the bike that I see is the one I see in my head. My thoughts have been realized into this object.

I'm starting to understand.

"Well done, Chance," Esri says. "Let's proceed a bit farther, shall we? Why haven't you ridden a motorcycle before?"

"I'm too young, and they're too dangerous."

"Dangerous?" Esri scoffs. "Is anything safe worth remembering? That's nonsense, Chance. I've witnessed kids half your age ride motorcycles all over the world, and they ride them well."

"Well, fine. But, I bet those kids don't have epilepsy. What if I have a seizure while driving that thing?"

"You tell me," he challenges.

"I'd crash, I guess."

"Shall we see?"

"What?" I ask.

"Go on. Let's see. Ride that bike, Chance. It's your creation"

"How?" I ask.

"How did it show up in the first place?" he asks.

"Oh, right," I say. I start to imagine riding the motorcycle. My thoughts skip over climbing onto the seat and starting the engine. Before I know it, I'm on the bike, accelerating and carving through curves in a road that has split the endless black horizon in two.

"Very nice," I hear Esri's voice. Once again, his words come from somewhere... nowhere... everywhere. I don't see him. I only see the road in front of me and the emptiness on each side of it. "Now what was that about motorcycles being dangerous? Why are they dangerous?"

"Because, they're fast," I say. "Very fast."

"How fast are they?" he asks.

"I've heard of bikes that can go 200 miles per hour," I say. The bike jolts forward. It picks up speed. I look down at the speedometer to see I'm already going 65. The top speed reads 200 mph.

"Is 200 miles per hour dangerous?" he asks.

"Yeah, I guess. I mean, it depends on the conditions and your experience and stuff like that."

"What type of conditions?" Esri asks.

"If you ride on tight curves, up mountain switchbacks, or something like that." I look up from the speedometer. A single mountain peak has appeared out of nowhere. A steep set of hairpin turns paves a path to the top. The bike speeds up. The needle pushes past 100 miles per hour. My mind wants to panic.

"How is this, Chance? Is this dangerous? How could you make it more dangerous, still?"

"Rain," I say, reluctantly. Immediately, drops splatter on the small windshield. The road ahead shines. It's slick. Very slick. The speedometer breaks 125 as I start up the curving hills.

"Yes, rain," Esri confirms. "That is dangerous. And what was that other bit that made riding especially dangerous for you, Chance?"

"Seizures?" I ask.

"Ah, yes. Seizures. What would happen if you had a seizure while going...let's see...oh you are up to 150 now? My, my. What will happen?"

In a flash, I disconnect from the Chance riding the motorcycle. I see a vision of myself starting to convulse. My body rides an out-of-control vehicle off the edge of a mountain road cliff. My mind freezes. I look below the falling body. Endless darkness awaits. This must be the end.

"Breathe, Chance," a calmer, more comforting Esri voice calls out. "Breathe. You aren't falling. Your body isn't even here. Remember?"

I look around. I need to find something familiar. "Esri, where are you? Where are you? Come here, please. Quick!"

"I'm here," I hear a voice in front of me call. Esri's figure appears and he paces towards me. "And your mind is here." Esri pauses for a moment, then continues. "There's no motorcycle. No mountain, no rain, no seizure. Those were all just thoughts. See how thoughts become reality in the Unseen?"

"Yeah," I say. "But, it wasn't exactly enjoyable. Couldn't we have started with something a little...easier?"

He waves a disapproving hand at me like he's batting a fly. "There's no learning, no progress, in *easy*."

"Fine," I say. I remain silent for a few moments. I need to process what's just happened. From entering the Unseen to creating a dream-bike with my mind alone, to watching myself fly off a cliff only to find out none of it was real in the first place. Or, was it all real but just didn't lead to any physical damage? I'm starting to understand, but I have a long way to go.

"But if it's all just thought in here," I start. "How can I actually impact other people back in the Seen. How can I check on Paul? How can I communicate with him?"

"Ah, yes," Esri replies. "That's it, exactly, Chance. That's why you are here, and that's why I came to find you. Your power, Chance... You span two worlds, unlike me. Unlike any Omnituen and most others who roam the Unseen."

"So, what do I do?"

"Not yet, Chance. We must take this slowly, or you'll wear yourself out both here and back in the Seen. I'm pleased to know you're ready to take next steps."

I'm not so sure. Am I ready?

Chapter 9

My eyes open involuntarily. I try to look around, but my head feels like it weighs hundreds of pounds. In fact, my whole body feels chained to the floor. I manage to roll my head to the side. Outside the treehouse window the sky is painted with strokes of gentle pink and orange, a standard summer sunset. I'm back in the Seen, surely. How long was I out? I hope it's the same day. If I have spent an entire night and another day out here...no, Mom and Dad would have come looking for me.

I should go inside and get ready for bed. I don't need my parents hawking over me now. This...this *power* of mine, it's going to take some getting used to. I need time on my own as well as uninterrupted time to spend with Esri in the Unseen without my parents wondering about me. But first things first; how do I get off the treehouse floor? I'm exhausted.

I roll my entire body to the side and try to push myself to an upright position. I fail with a crash to the floor. My face hits first, but fortunately it only fell a couple of inches. Can this possibly be worth it? Unseen aside, is risking more seizures worth it?

I'm not so sure.

If it truly means getting Paul back, then yes, it's worth it. I use that potential as encouragement to get off the floor. I'm up on all fours now. I crawl to the opening in the floor. As I slowly climb down the ladder, I try to piece together what's happened since I last left the house. The events from the Unseen are clear. But I still don't understand how that Unseen world will help me find Paul. Even if I can find him, how will I get him back home?

I shake my head to dislodge these unwelcome thoughts. Not a good idea. That little movement shoots pain between my ears and knocks me off balance. I bend to kneel on the ground and rest against the bottom ladder rung. I take some breaths and wait for the discomfort to subside. I look up at the tree. It would be nice to see Esri. He might have some suggestions on how to deal with this.

He isn't there.

I pull myself to my feet and turn my head towards the kitchen window. Mom hasn't cleaned up dinner. She still sits there, staring at a half-eaten meal. Dad isn't in the room. I take some big breaths and let go of the ladder. I start the most difficult journey I've ever taken from the treehouse to the house. I feel like a baby deer taking its first steps. I manage to move, but I'm sure it looks ridiculous.

"Please don't look out the window," I whisper, hoping that somehow Mom obeys a voice she cannot hear.

"Make a note of this for next time," I tell myself. If this is how I'm going to feel after every trip to the Unseen, I need to be prepared. I continue across the backyard, and I can't stop questioning everything. Do I want to keep doing this? What is the point? Mom and Dad seem pleased with their conversation with the General. Isn't it best to wait and see, at least for a few days?

I reach the house. Before I enter, I peer through the kitchen window again. Mom stares at her plate. Her eyes are unfocused, though, and she doesn't seem to notice what's happening around her. It's like she isn't really there. She's with Paul. Rather, she wishes she could be with Paul.

Maybe she's mad that her thoughts can't bring him back. But mine can. Maybe. I'm not so sure.

I ready myself for acting like nothing significant has happened since I last saw my parents. I open the back door. Before joining Mom in the kitchen, I wiggle my limbs a few times. I try to look awake. I comb my hair with my fingers. I take another deep breath and enter the kitchen.

I catch Mom off guard. "Hey, hon," she says. "I didn't hear you come in. Restful time in the treehouse?"

"Yeah," I say.

She focuses more intently on my face. She furrows her brow. "Chance, are you OK?"

"Yeah, of course," I say. "Just a little tired."

She purses her lips and twists them to the side of her mouth. She doesn't believe me. That's obvious. But she lets it go.

"OK," she says. "Best get some rest then, huh?" She must not have the energy to question me further.

Before I can agree and retreat to my room, Dad bursts into the kitchen. His voice and movement exude more energy than this house has felt in days.

"Look, look," he says. He holds up an envelope. "A letter. From Paul."

He sits down at the table and tears open the envelope. I take the seat next to him, and Mom scoots her chair to his other side. We read the letter together:

> mom and pops,
> good news. i'm still fine. they have us going through some qretty tough exercises and testing, but everything is good. the general told us about the letter thinq. kinda weird that they'd do that, but i get it. qarents must have been worried and i'm sure he wanted to let everybody know we're OK. anyway, he said from now on, we would write the letters. so, here i am. writing the letter. it qrobably will be a while before i write again. we are getting ready to go through the enhancement qrocess. it takes a few days to qrep our bodies for enhancement, and then a few days to go through the qrocedure. then, it takes a week or so to recover. obviously, they need to make sure they concentrate on keeqing us healthy and safe, and they don't want stuff from back home to interfere with any of that.

so, just know i'm good. we're all good. i do miss you though. Chance too. tell him i said so. love you guys. see you before you know it.

love,
P

We sit in silence. At first, we keep our mouths shut to give each other time to read. At some point, it's clear everyone has finished reading. Now we just don't know what to say.

Maybe we're not willing to accept that this *enhancement* is a simple procedure. Each of us knows it's serious. We know it's never been done before. At least it's comforting to read Paul's words and know that they're his this time. We know he's alive. That's encouraging. But his letter screams a terrifying reality. The government isn't treating him as an American hero. He's nothing more than an experiment. A guinea pig. A crash test dummy.

If Paul were coming home soon, maybe we wouldn't be so uneasy about his lab rat status. But his letter contradicts what General Palmer told my parents. Paul's letter described weeks and weeks...and more weeks.

Paul isn't coming home for a while. We're being lied to. What else don't we know?

Maybe we've put a false hope in simply hearing from my brother. When Dad showed it to the family, excitement and relief were natural. But now that we have some time to digest what Paul wrote, his words raise more questions than they provide answers. That feeling of unknown is creeping back. It's sinking in. Mom's blank face returns. Dad's hands start to fidget again. The hopelessness of the unknown is back. Will it ever go away?

I'm not so sure.

My brother has been ripped from us. He's about to undergo an unprecedented medical procedure. A procedure that isn't going to fix a problem. There's nothing wrong with Paul. He's perfect just the way he is. But against his family's will, those more powerful than us have decided he can be more useful if they make him *different*. And his family, those who love him most, will just be an interference, a nuisance, to the overall mission if we see or talk to him now. It isn't fair. There's nothing we can do about it.

Eventually, Mom mumbles: "P's and q's."

"Yeah," Dad says. "That's our boy. He's still OK."

I'm not so sure.

Who should I believe: General Palmer? Esri? Someone else? For now, I know two things: first, my parents aren't going to talk about the letter or the situation in front of me; second, I need some rest. Everyone can agree on that.

I need to get out of this kitchen. The longer Mom and Dad hold back their true feelings, the more they morph into people I don't recognize.

I break the silence. "Yeah," I say. "He's still OK. I'm going to head upstairs and get some rest."

My legs feel like sandbags. Each step takes concentrated effort. The staircase looks like Mt. Everest. I take one painful step at a time. Each time I lift one leg, the other feels like it will collapse under the pressure of the rest of my body. How can a thought-world zap so much physical energy? Finally, I arrive at my bedroom door. I pause to listen if Mom and Dad have started talking.

Silence. They're waiting for me to be out of earshot.

I shut my door loudly, so they can hear it. But I stay in the hallway. The close of my door acts like a dam breaking. Mom bursts into tears. Her cries are quickly muffled when she buries her head into Dad's embrace.

"What are we going to do?" she weeps to him.

"Shhhhh," Dad tries to comfort her. "I don't know. I don't know yet. But we're going to figure something out. We will get him back. We will get him back."

Knowing how they truly feel, I quietly open my door, creep inside, and close it silently behind me. I want to help. I think maybe I know how to help. Maybe Esri and the Unseen are the best way. The worst part will be hiding it from them.

Part of me is ready to take the leap that Esri has been urging me to take since I first met him. Part of me hopes Dad will come up with an idea. Maybe he will figure out where the General is keeping Paul and the others. I know he's already looking into it. He is always a step ahead of everyone else when it comes to solving problems. It doesn't matter the scope or size: Dad solves problems.

I need someone to talk to, someone to help me work this out. I need Paul. He isn't here. He isn't going to be here until this is all worked out. I come close to my bed. My body knows where it is. It collapses onto the mattress.

For now, I need to stay healthy. That starts with sleep. My parents and Esri, although they will never meet, undoubtedly see eye to eye on that point.

Chapter 10

I wake up groggy, but without a headache. I'm thankful for that. I mosey downstairs to what sounds like an empty house. I look in each room, but I see no one. I peek into the kitchen to see if Mom and Dad left a note.

Nothing.

It's nothing to panic about. I'm old enough to stay home by myself. It's just a little weird that they didn't let me know where they are. Actually, it's kind of nice they aren't home. I won't have to hide my next trip to the Unseen. Although, how can I hide it? I don't know what happens to my body when I travel to the Unseen. I ponder that reality for a moment. It's too much to process. I need some food, and I need to get back to the treehouse.

I grab a granola bar from the pantry and start towards the backdoor. Before I grip the knob, Mom comes in through the door that leads to the garage. With the door open, I hear a car backing out of the driveway.

"Oh, good morning," she says. I've surprised her. She hurries the door shut, maybe to muffle the sound of a quickly departing car. "You're up early." She fakes a smile. I'm getting sick of the forced smiles around here. They don't need to hide their fear from me. "Did you sleep well? How are you feeling?"

I don't want to stick around for this conversation. I need to get back to the treehouse. Only one answer will get me out of this quickly: "Yeah. I slept well. I feel fine."

"Good," she says. "Do you want some breakfast?"

"I have a granola bar. I'm going to eat it in the treehouse."

"OK," she says. "Have fun. Your dad will probably be gone for a few days. So it's just you and me. If you get hungry or want to go out and have some fun, let me know."

I stare at her. Should I ask what's going on? Does she want me to ask? Dad's obviously trying to find Paul, but Mom looks like she's about to unravel. She grimaces, trying to hold herself together. Should I stay here and pull information out of her? Slowly. Tearfully. Or should I go to the treehouse and keep training? I'm still half asleep. I can't make a decision. I opt for the easy way out.

"Yeah, OK," I say.

"Great. Have fun, honey."

I walk to the treehouse, breakfast in hand. I climb the ladder. I hear Esri the moment I sit down.

"Your father's off, no?"

"Geez," I scoff. "You don't always have to be so *in your face*. And are you always going to be reading my mind now?"

"Ah, 'in your face,' you say. Tell me, did you come up here *not* to see me?"

"Huh?" I ask.

"Nevermind, I suppose. Regarding your mind, and my reading it. Yes. I will be reading your mind. But only reading the thoughts that *you* need to know. Will that be a problem, Chance?"

"What does that even mean?" I ask. "Thoughts that *I* need to know. They're my thoughts. I think I know them." I take a bite of my bar and turn away acting more frustrated than I actually am. "And yes, that might be a problem."

Esri brushes his hand in front of his face, batting flies again. "Ah, stop it. Stop it. Shall we proceed already?"

"Can I eat my breakfast?" I snap back.

He raises a knuckle to his lips, as if that will seal them shut. He moves his hand further up his face and pinches the bridge of his nose. "I've introduced you to a world where anything and everything is readily available at the mere thought of it. But you, you want me to wait for you to finish a snack bar?"

"I can't eat it once we get to the Unseen, so yes, I do want you to wait."

He turns away from me and begins to pace down the tree branch. He continues to squeeze his forehead between his thumb and forefinger. Me frustrating him is going to be a standard aspect of our relationship.

"Oh simple one," he says. "How long will you love being simple?"

"There, I'm done," I answer, my mouth full. "Was that so hard? I'm ready to get started."

Esri lifts a finger and opens his mouth. He seems to change his mind, though, and he snaps his lips shut. An argument isn't worth the time.

"Yes, let's begin."

I smile as if I've won an argument, but he glares his disagreement and continued disapproval.

His arm lifts as it had before. I prepare my eyes for the standard starlight show. However, as soon as my fist touches his, I'm immediately in the Unseen. In the darkness. No nerves. No stars. Just the Unseen.

"What happened?" I ask.

"You're learning," Esri's voice replies. His figure appears in the distance and starts walking towards me. "Your energy. You're learning to use it to cross from the Seen to the Unseen instead of pushing your body into convulsions. I tell you the truth when I say there's power in your...what did you call it *disability*.'"

"OK," I say. I look down at my feet. The ripples appear. This time they're blue. My body is fully visible. Some part of my mind seems to be a few steps ahead of me. I guess that's possible.

"It's all possible, Chance," Esri interrupts. "Conscious or sub-conscious, you are fully here and engaged."

"Oh yeah, mind reading. I forgot."

"Is there anything other than our thoughts?" he asks. I don't answer. Does he want me to answer?

"What's next?" I ask.

"Training," he replies. "You've learned to cross from the Seen to the Unseen. Each trip is smoother than the last. That's good. But now, you must learn to navigate through the Unseen. To do so, you must master your thoughts. Use them to go where you need to go."

"But—"

"Ah, I know." Esri barely lets me start the sentence. "Thoughts: your archenemy for as long as you can remember. A neverending stress creator. The primary culprit for the episodes back in the Seen. I know."

He pauses and waits for me to reply. Why would I reply? He already knows what I'm thinking.

He smirks and continues: "We'll progress slowly...relatively. Time is of the essence. Shall we begin with positive, peaceful thoughts?"

I nod.

"It's a shame you insisted on eating that blasted bar. Hunger is generally a harmless thought-invoking feeling, but I suppose it's not readily available to you at the moment."

"I thought there weren't any feelings in here, Esri," I say. "How can I *feel* hunger."

"Exactly," Esri says. His eyes widen. He's a little too excited. "The feelings aren't real, but you are already an expert at navigating with senses. Utilize those years of experience with senses here in the Unseen. If you want to move, your mind will find it easy to walk or get on a motorcycle as you did yesterday. If you want food to eat, your mind can easily drum up a feeling of hunger. Your mind isn't used to working without senses, so use what's familiar, and your experience will take over. These feelings, as you say, won't always be necessary, but they will help here at the beginning. But beware, senses can be overly intense when created in your mind.

"Nevertheless," Esri continues. "Despite your insistence on eating the bar, can you imagine hunger? Shall we say you haven't eaten in three days? Does that spark an emptiness in your gut?"

I close my eyes and imagine his direction. Three days ago. Wednesday. I think about eating dinner with Mom and Dad. We had spaghetti. Suddenly, I'm there at the table with Mom and Dad. I hear Mom's voice:

"Chance, could you pass the bread please."

I hear some muffled version of my own voice acknowledge her request. I respond, but I can't understand the words. It's like my voice projects from a speaker that's been turned upside down. I can tell it's me at my typical spot at the table, but I can't make out any details. I see only a blurry silhouette of a kid my age. Mom and Dad don't appear fazed by my appearance. I must look normal to them.

"Yes," Esri encourages. "Now, assume that was the last time that you ate. It's been almost three entire days since that meal. You've had nothing to eat since then."

My mouth waters. My stomach rumbles. I feel *feelings* for the first time in the Unseen. And they are intense. They're more real than anything I've felt before. I can't concentrate on anything other than the fact that *I AM HUNGRY*. How can hunger hurt this bad?

"Your thoughts are reality here, Chance." Esri is mind reading again. "They are realized fully and completely. Hurtful thoughts will be excruciatingly painful. But the converse is true. What would you like to eat now, Chance?"

The pain is gripping. I can't make any decisions. "Anything. Anything. A granola bar. Just, give me a granola bar!"

There. In my hand. A granola bar appears. I cram it into my mouth and devour it. The hunger pangs reside as I swallow the last dry bit.

"Relax," Esri says. "Now, what's your favorite food, Chance?"

"Tacos."

A table forms in front of me. It extends beyond eyesight in both directions. A taco bar waits for me to dive in. Ground beef, chicken, steak...what's that? Is it carnitas? That's what I've always imagined carnitas to be, but I've never seen them. Every topping I have ever witnessed, or even pondered, overflows containers: salsas, pickled vegetables, guacamole, nuts, and cheese. Oh, look at the cheese. Shredded cheese, cubed cheese, silky queso, more queso, buckets of queso. Is a taco really anything more than a vehicle to get cheese into your belly? I had once wondered if chocolate chips would be good on a taco. Sure enough, at least six different types of chocolate chips sit on the table waiting for me to build the taco of my dreams.

It doesn't end with the tacos. A tiled floor appears just under my feet replacing the ripples. The new floor extends to the table and then spreads the length of the taco bar. Pinatas and colorful banners suddenly hang overhead. The spicy smell of chiles and the smokey aroma of grilled meat fills the air around me. I take it in with a deep breath. Then another. The distant sound of a guitar glides through the atmosphere and bounces off the checkered floor. I've joined the most magnificent Tex- Mex feast ever imagined.

"What are you waiting for?" Esri interrupts.

My eyes meet his. He chuckles at my amazement and encourages, "Dig in. It's for the taking."

I make my go-to: hardshell ground beef taco with queso. I scarf it down. Before I finish chewing, I eye the table for my next creation. I try a soft taco with chicken and cheese. I build a

taco salad with steak, queso, and shredded lettuce. I don't even like lettuce, but why not? Before I had finished half of the salad, I start plans for a fourth helping.

My mouth full, I ask Esri, "Aren't you going to have some?"

He holds up a hand to politely decline. "It would quarrel with sound wisdom to seek such desire."

I don't understand what he means, but he seemed sincere. I don't want to argue. I want to eat tacos. So I eat until I feel ready to burst.

"Full, then?" Esri asks.

"Yep. If that's all it takes to fulfill my meaning in the Unseen, then I'm ready to go."

Esri starts to fake a smile, but quickly moves on. "Satisfying a painful appetite gives you a sense of the power within this place. Don't dwell on this, but imagine pains worse than appetite. Imagine pleasures greater than your favorite food. The Unseen is infinitely vast both in substance and captivation. When I say many have lost themselves here, that's no exaggeration. You must be careful, and we must go slowly. Assure me you understand that, Chance."

His eyes pierce mine, demanding an answer. "I guess so," I reply.

His eyes narrow. His glare commands honesty.

"Well, I'm not sure," I correct myself. "I've only just arrived here, but I don't see how I could lose touch with the Seen. If I think about sleeping, I still want to go back to my bed to fall asleep. I still love my family, and I want to go back to them. I'm not sure how this place can help me connect to or right any wrongs in the Seen." I pause for a moment. I want to make sure I've put everything out there. "And, that's it, I think. That's the honest truth. That's what I'm thinking."

"Alright," he says. The tension in his temples relaxes. Again, I forget he already knows what I'm thinking, but I guess he needs me to be intentionally honest with all of my thoughts and emotions. It's such a strange place.

"Let's proceed," he says. "See some things, shall we?"

"OK."

The taco bar vanishes. The building. The guitar tunes. The delicious smells. They're all gone. The most inviting scene I've experienced in the Unseen is replaced with unnerving emptiness.

Esri walks away into endless darkness. No ripples dance around his feet. No objects wait in front of him. He walks into nothingness. I hesitate to catch up to him. I want the feast back. But I don't want to lose him. I don't want to be alone.

"Follow me," he says. My feet start moving. I don't consciously make them move. I'm a remote control car, and Esri's voice is the controller. I catch up and we start gliding towards...nowhere.

Why aren't my nerves heating up? My stomach should be grabbing. I pat my pants pocket for a pill that isn't there.

"It'll be there if you so desire it," Esri says without breaking course.

"Oh, yeah. I forgot."

"Acknowledge your thoughts, Chance. Infinite darkness should make a human scared. It's only natural. Accept your fear, and let it pass by."

"Right. OK."

I turn my head all around and let the black surround me. Cover me. Consume me. Whenever we stop talking, fear starts to creep its fingers around my arms, my legs, my throat.

"Tell me how you feel, Chance," Esri says.

"I feel scared, like I'm choking."

"Indeed, good," he replies, stone faced.

"What?" How is that good?

"Let the fear come, Chance. Let it wash right over you."

I shake my shoulders and my head. My breath shortens. The breaths are too quick to count. My face gets hot. My chest tightens. What is the air made of in here? Why is it so hard to breathe?

"Let it go, Chance!" His voice startles me, and somehow the breath is scared back into me.

"What was that?" I ask. "Just talk. Please keep talking. It helps when you talk."

"So long as you fear it, it will control you. You stop fearing the Unseen when I talk because you are distracted. You need to learn to deal with the fear without me. Without my voice. Without distractions."

"OK, how?" I ask.

"How do you learn anything? Practice."

"OK, let's go. I'm good now."

"Your body back in the Seen is exhausted. Your energy, the energy that previously sustained seizures for a minute or two at a time... It's kept you here, connected to the Unseen for...a while. We'll proceed tomorrow."

I blink. I'm back on the treehouse floor. Again, the weight of my body pins me to the floorboards. This time, Esri has stuck around for me to wake up.

"Awake, young Chance?" he asks. "Yeah, I'm here."

"Ah, yes. And how do you feel?"

"Terrible."

"Ah. Good."

"What?" I ask. "Why?"

Esri glances away. He rubs his temples, drumming up a thought. "I've said you have a gift, a power. I've not said your path to realizing your potential will be easy. On the contrary, it will be difficult, likely the most excruciating experience of your life."

I look at him, confused. He stops talking and shakes his head. He pinches the bridge of his nose again and ponders his next words.

"Perseverance is essential to achieving any goal worth its name. But for more immediate purposes, you must fight to keep normalcy here in the Seen. Your parents must see you as rested and healthy. You can't afford them to come looking for you while you're in the Unseen or pushing you full of pills that knock you out for a week. Pick yourself up off the floor. Get inside. Put on a brave face. Endure. When you feel you can't move another inch, move two. And remember Paul. He needs you."

The sound of his voice exhausts me more. I grimace when I turn my head to face him. My frustration disappoints him.

"Fine," I concede. "Help me up?"

"I can't. I don't exist in this world."

Chapter 11

When I wake up, my body begs me to go back to sleep. Esri was right: I feel like I could sleep another twelve hours, but my mind fights my body. It's had a taste of the Unseen and its potential. That sample lures me back. I want more training. I want to see more. I want to experience how I might help find my brother through the Unseen. I ignore my slothlike body and throw the covers back. I jump up and rush around my room to get dressed. I move with a sense of purpose that's foreign to me. I have something to look forward to. And that potential, it blots out the fear that has so far defined this summer.

I open my bedroom door. The house is silent again. Dad must still be gone. Maybe Mom is out running errands. It's a perfect opportunity to slip downstairs and outside without any questions. I bound down the stairs and walk past the kitchen. I'm nearly to the back door when Mom's voice calls me back.

"Good morning, hon," she says. I stop short of the backdoor and backstep to the kitchen threshold.

"Hey, good morning," I say.

"Where are you headed?" She sounds distracted. It's like her question was read off of a notecard instead of asked out of interest. She knows where I'm going. I've spent most of the summer break in the treehouse. Before school ended, all I talked about was spending more time in the treehouse. Before I answer, I take a long look at her. She isn't even looking at me. She stares straight ahead at the kitchen wall.

I take one step into the kitchen. She doesn't move. I walk towards her. I reach the table and ease my way into the seat across from her. She doesn't break her stare at the wall. She looks just to the outside of my left ear. I survey her face. Mascara streaks have bled down her cheeks. She sniffles in regular intervals, again and again. Her hair is tied back in a ponytail. She never wears her hair in a ponytail.

What is wrong?

I don't know what to say. I've never seen her like this. I'm typically the one needing to be comforted; it's Mom who's always there to comfort me. She's the best at it. I don't know where to begin. Words escape me. I stare at her until she finally breaks her gaze on her own.

Her eyes meet mine.

"Good morning, hon," she robotically repeats herself. "What are you up to?"

What has happened to my mother?

Seeing her stare at the wall was bad, but the lifeless eye contact is worse. She needs help. I can't offer any. At least not here in the Seen. I try to act like I can't tell something is wrong. That's what Mom and Dad do when they don't want me to know something's off. I hope I'm not as obvious as they are.

"I'm just headed to the treehouse for a bit," I say. "Maybe read or something. I don't know. We'll see. Have you heard from Dad? When's he coming home?"

Tears fill her eyes. Why did I ask that question?

"I'm sure it won't be too much longer, Mom," I try to reassure her. "The General said it wouldn't be too much longer, and with Dad out searching, I bet he'll get better answers before we even hear from Paul or the General, again. Don't you think? I'm sure that's the case."

I should stop talking. She can't handle this. I'm making it worse

She rests her face in her hands. Her entire body starts to shake. She fights back sobs which leads to giant, silent full-body spasms. She doesn't want me to hear or see her upset. I need to let her know I'm OK.

I walk around the table to her side. I put my arms around her. "It's OK to be scared, Mom. We're only human. We're supposed to be scared when loved ones are taken away."

She continues to shake. Short, uncontrollable cries break through her fight to hold back tears.

"We can't live in fear," I add. "If we live in fear, the fear controls us. And it wins. We can't let it win, right?"

She lifts her face from her hands. She looks me straight in the eyes. For the first time that morning, maybe the first time since school ended, she sees me. She finally sees...me.

"Where did you hear that?" she asks.

"I don't know," I lie. I guess Esri has more effect on the Seen than he knows. Or, maybe just more than he's willing to let me know.

For the moment, Mom seems OK. That's enough for me. I hug her again. I don't want to let her go. But the Unseen calls. There's work to be done.

"You good?" I ask.

"Yeah, good," she affirms. "Thanks, Chance. Have some fun out there. It's been a tough summer. But, we'll be OK."

I walk out the backdoor with my head held high. Ready for training. Ready to help get my brother back. I still have no idea how it will work. But I'm ready to learn.

I poke my head through the treehouse floor. Esri waits inside. He sits on the windowsill. Our eyes meet. We each know the other is ready. Without a word, he holds up his fist. I walk over and push my fist against his.

I blink involuntarily. A powerful flash of light washes out everything in my field of vision. Then, there's total darkness. Once again, I'm surrounded by blackness. Ripples around my feet, this time purple, are the only color I see. I turn in a circle, searching for Esri. Eventually, I notice him walking twenty or thirty yards in front of me. He moves away from me. Before chasing after him, I think about my options to catch up. Instead of running after him, I force my mind to imagine him coming to me instead of me going to him.

We're side by side. My thoughts...worked. He tries to hold back a grin. "Well done. Shall we?"

I don't answer, but instead I think: *Ready as ever.*

His smile creeps through again: "Good."

We walk forward. The black, horizonless scene in front of us remains empty as far as we can see. It's unnerving walking into nothingness. Each new step feels like it might be the one that finally leads me over a cliff: a cliff I can't see. We continue our trek until that constant fear of falling subsides. I'm starting to feel just a bit comfortable when I hear faint sounds in the distance. It sounds like birds. Sea birds. I hear a shoreline, the smallest waves breaking on a beach.

Then, blurred colors appear a few hundred yards in front of us. I see the divide of land and water, but the colors are muted and the horizon unclear. It's like walking through an impressionist painting. I look down. We're walking on...water.

I prepare myself to break through the water's surface and start swimming. But I don't fall through. The water comes into clear focus, and I look back up to the shoreline. Now, the entire landscape appears in high definition. Esri and I walk on a huge body of water towards the shore. The water is glassy. I look at Esri. He doesn't seem fazed by this impossible feat. His demeanor reassures me.

I look back across the water. The beach is closer than before. I can be there in five or ten seconds if I run. I pick up the pace. As I speed up, a city bursts through the earth just beyond the sandy beach. It's how I've pictured mountains violently forming during massive earthquakes. But instead of jagged rock peaks, this quake thrusts modern buildings, gigantic trees, and an entire city skyline into the air. A flawless city, one I've never dreamed of, fills the scene as far as I can see. I look around, the black is gone. It's city in front of me and water behind.

The cityscape is expertly crafted with architectural masterpieces. The buildings include perfectly curved sides and diamond-precise edges. They shine with hues of crystal, gold, and silver. But the city is more than buildings. Interwoven between them, lush gardens grow, and a glass-clear river flows through the metropolis. Out of the gardens, skyscraper-sized trees match the size and grandeur of the highrises. From the trees, vine- constructed bridges connect the forest to the buildings and the buildings to each other. It's Eden reborn in a modern urban setting.

We stop walking when we reach the edge of the city. To our left, an enormous sports stadium that appears to be carved from one mammoth piece of marble begs our attention. Esri nods in its direction. We start towards it. The river that carves its way throughout the city flows beside us, also on its way to the stadium. As we near the marble structure, a tower rises out of the ground, much the way the buildings had first appeared when we approached the city. The tower looks to be a cylindrical block of ice a few hundred feet tall. As we come closer, I notice rusty rebar rungs sticking out of the ice block. They create a rickety ladder that spans the entire height of the structure.

The river that runs alongside us now widens and turns on the other side of the ice tower. It separates the tower, where we have now stopped, from the behemoth stadium. I look up. A vine bridge spans the river. It connects the ice tower to the stadium. I imagine what it would take to climb that ladder and cross that bridge. I swallow down the lump in my throat.

"What's this?" I ask.

"This is your training ground, Chance."

I don't know what he means, but the comment evokes a brand new sense of unease.

"You crawl. Then you walk. Then you run. Eventually, you communicate. And, if needed, you fight."

I assume these are metaphors of some sort. But I don't know what they mean. Before I have time to ponder their meaning, a sharp pain shoots through my legs. My face hits the ground. I lay on my stomach. I try to get my arms underneath me to push myself off the ground.

"See you in the stadium," Esri says. He disappears.

From the ground, I look up at the stadium. My eyes find the bridge that connects the stadium to the tower. The pillar of ice appears to be melting. I spring to my feet. I need to get to that bridge before it all collapses.

As soon as my feet hit the ground, ice from the tower spreads like spilled oil across the ground towards me. I'm instantly surrounded by a sheet of ice. I can't move an inch without slipping. I test a cautious step forward. The ice crawls up my feet and grabs my ankles. My legs are frozen stiff. They won't budge.

What's going on? What am I supposed to do? "What did he say?" I ask myself. "He said, crawl, walk That's it!"

I fall back to my stomach. The ice releases its grip from my legs. I curl my knees under me, and rise to a crawling position. The ice that blankets the ground around me begins to retreat. I slowly crawl toward the tower and grab the first ladder rung.

The first bar feels strong, so I pull myself to my feet and start to climb. I pause about ten feet into my ascent. I look up the frozen column. It continues to melt, and steel bars sporadically fall away as the melting ice loses its grip of the ladder. "It's in your head," I tell myself and climb on.

Slowly and cautiously, I make my way to the bridge. The viney crossover looks less sturdy up close. My body shakes. I rise to my feet. The bridge between the tower and the stadium looks to be about two hundred yards long. Gaping holes break the bridge into sections. The gaps require a jump to cross. There's no other way. I need a running start if I'm going to complete the first leap.

I take a deep breath and try to spring forward like a sprinter out of a starting block. The moment I move, vines grab my front foot. Another set of vines grab the other leg, up to my knee. My body crashes into the viney surface which makes the entire bridge sway. I squeeze my eyes shut, and hope the swinging stops. When I finally stop swaying, I open my eyes. My face hangs over an open space in the bridge. I stare down at the ground. It's hundreds of feet below, but it feels like thousands. My body seizes. I grasp the first two vines I can find. The living bridge violently reacts. Vines increase their vice grip on my legs. I turn my head and avoid looking at the fall below me.

I take a few deep breaths and think more about Esri's instruction: "Walk....That's next."

Maybe these aren't metaphors. I'm going to learn this place like I learned the Seen world, just like a baby. I think about walking, and the vines loosen from my legs. Another set of vines approach and then cradle me. They hug my entire body and lift me to my feet. I look across the bridge. The holes are still there. How am I supposed to get across without jumping?

I consider my next move. It's all in my head. The elaborate city that fills the space around me, the stadium, the vine bridge, it can all be controlled by my mind. I breathe and let that sink in. Steps in the Seen require my legs. Steps in the Unseen require my mind.

I close my eyes and envision myself walking across the bridge, straight across the open holes. But committing to that thought with my eyes open is a different story. What happens if I fall through? I shuffle back to the edge of the hole. I peek down at the ground.

The ground has disappeared. Where will I fall to? There's nothing down there.

"That's right," I tell myself. "There's nothing down there, Chance. But, there's nothing up here either if you don't want there to be. You can walk wherever you want. You can do this."

I take a deep breath. I focus my eyes towards the end of the bridge. I step forward onto the open space. My foot should have fallen through the gap. Instead, flowering vines fill the space and the sole of my foot rolls with a step just as natural as any I have ever taken. I continue to walk across the bridge. I shed a little more worry with each stride.

I step off of the bridge and enter the outer halls of the stadium. I have crawled and walked. Running is obviously next. But to where? And why? Esri said he would see me *in the stadium*. I must find a way to the center.

I start around the outer concourse, looking for a tunnel into the middle. I walk a few paces and I hear cracking. I turn in the direction where the sound originates. In front of me, a boulder-sized chunk of marble falls. It shatters on the floor where I had been walking just seconds before. The dust starts to clear, and I hear more cracks. I look up and see another slab of the upper deck starting to give way.

"I guess I start running now," I say. I bolt away from the crumbling arena.

I spot an exit around the next curve. I look over my shoulder.

Stadium sections collapse in succession. The demolition picks up speed. If I sprint as fast as I can, I will probably make the exit before being crushed. I sprint, all my attention focused on the exit.

"Keep your mind focused on the exit," I tell myself. If I focus on getting to the exit, it will become a reality. That's how it works in here.

"In the stadium," Esri's voice drowns out the sound of collapsing stone. I keep running. "The instruction was to meet *in* the stadium." Still running, I start to process his words. He doesn't want me to run away from the wreckage. He wants me to run towards it, into it.

"You've got to be kidding me." I can barely speak. I try to catch my breath.

I know what must be done. I turn towards the falling blocks. They domino towards me on a warpath.

"Here we go." I flee into the carnage with the recklessness of a madman and the conviction of a soldier.

I run into blinding dust. Excruciating thunder pummels my ear drums. I can vaguely see a rock wall in front of me. There's no way around it. As I approach what must be the end of my road, I catch a glimpse of a stadium chunk accelerating towards me from above. I brace for impact.

But, I don't feel the slightest pain. I open my eyes. Dust flies everywhere. I wave my hand to brush it away. It starts to clear, slowly. Then, like a puff of air blowing out a candle, the particles all vanish.

It's back to black. No ground. No sky. No city. Emptiness. I wait for him to show up. Surely, he'll show up any second. He always does.

I wait longer. Nothing. The silence plays on until a stinging ring replaces it. My ears ache. What is going on? It annoys me more than anything. What's next? Let's get on with it. I want to get the dust off of me and keep moving forward.

"OK, fine," I say out loud. "I get it. If I want it, I make it happen. Is that right?" I yell into the void.

I imagine the dust fleeing my body like dandelion seeds away from the stem. I look at my arms, then my legs. Clean as a whistle. I imagine a glass of water; after all, I've run a lot. I must be thirsty. In front of me, a tall glass of water appears on a table.

"If you aren't going to show up, I'll just take a seat on this couch," I arrogantly yell to Esri. I confidently throw my legs out, knowing a couch will appear below me. It does, and in the same moment, Esri appears and kicks it out from under me. I slam to the ground and blue ripples rush away from the outline of my body.

"Hey!" I say. "What was that?"

"First you crawled. Then you walked. Then you ran."

"That's not what I meant."

"Ah, yes. Then you fell, as the proud always do."

"So, I noticed," I bark.

"Your thoughts are power in here, Chance. But, your thoughts aren't the only thoughts in the Unseen. Remember that."

Chapter 12

I fight through exhaustion and post-Unseen aches and pains on my way back to my house. The sun starts to set. I must have fallen asleep in the treehouse after my trip this morning, but I'm still tired. I welcome the thought that bedtime is near. Just before I enter the house, I hear a car pull into the driveway. It's Dad. I know it's Dad. He's back. That has to be good news.

All traces of fatigue flee my body. I rush inside to meet him. Mom hears me throw the door open. "Chance, are you OK? What is it?"

"Dad's home! Didn't you hear the car?"

"No, really? Well, come on." She starts towards the garage. I follow. Before we reach it, Dad enters.

Mom throws herself at him. I try to wrap my arms around both of them. My arms aren't long enough, but it doesn't matter. I'm just glad to see him.

"Dad, you're home!" I exclaim.

"Yeah, I am. I missed you, bud. I missed you both." He kisses the top of Mom's head. We pile into the kitchen and sit down together.

"What did you find out?" I ask. "Did you find out more about

Paul? Anything?"

He doesn't answer. The group hug breaks up. Dad looks at me. He starts to answer, but bounces his eyes to Mom. Her eyes, eager as mine, wait anxiously. I thought his return would be good news, but now I'm not so sure.

"Joseph?" Mom asks.

"Yeah, well...No. I didn't find anything out," Dad admits. "We'll just have to stay patient. I'm sure we'll get another letter soon, or maybe—" His voice trails off. There's nothing left to say. He's just guessing.

Mom stays silent, her eyes locked on Dad's. She sees something I don't. Is Dad hiding something? Dad looks back at me. "Or maybe we'll have another video chat or press conference." His eyes keep bouncing back to Mom as he tries to comfort me. They need me to leave so they can speak freely. I'm sick of this. They don't know that I can actually help now. Not only am I *OK*, I'm actually getting stronger.

Or are you?

Or am I? I'm not so sure.

Sure, I've learned a thing or two in the Unseen. Esri, who's frustratingly difficult to please, has started admitting my progress. But that's the Unseen. This is the Seen. This is my parents' reality. And for the most part, this is still my reality. Here, I'm the opposite of who I am in the Unseen. I'm far from powerful. Here, I'm... disabled. Powerless. My parents hide basic truths from me, not because it's top secret or anything. They hide it because they fear the slightest disappointment will send me into an episode. They aren't even wrong for thinking that way. Not so long ago I had to check out of the world for a week just because I learned Paul was leaving for the summer. Does any amount of power in a thought-world offset my weakness here?

I'm not so sure.

Esri has tried to convince me that the Unseen is a truer reality. In that dimension, I'll somehow reach my full potential. But how can that be true when I'm still so helpless here in my own home? My parents have to protect me from the smallest dangers. Most people don't consider a little bit of news dangerouss at all, but to me stress is a poison that sets off a panicked chain reaction. My parents, my doctors, and everyone who cares for me leaps into emergency mode if I even get a little frustrated.

"Chance, it's going to be OK," Dad interrupts my thoughts and steals another uneasy look at Mom. "We just have to be patient."

"Yeah, be patient," I concede. "Well, I'm glad you're home. Is there anything I can do to help?" It was a rhetorical question. I know they don't want my help.

"Yes," he says. My ears perk up. "You can continue to stay calm and get plenty of rest."

"Perfect," I think, sarcastically. "The only way I can help is to stay out of the way. What a help I am."

Dad gently raises his arm, and holds my face in his hand. "I mean it, Chance. We're going to figure this out. You staying rested is the best thing for us. That includes Paul. It's the best thing you can do to help get Paul back." He smiles, but it's not a happy smile; It's a *I'm Dad and I know best* smile. Maybe he does know best. But I'm not so sure.

I retreat to my room. Less than an hour ago I had a spring in my step. I was excited that Dad was home, eager to help in my own unique way. But his words, his hiding the truth from me, it has taken all the energy out of my body. It hurts. The physical toll of the Unseen and the reality of my role in this world weigh on me. The stairs to my room feel like a path to a dungeon. I'm not going to rest in there. Sure, I'll be out of the way but I won't avoid stress. I'll do nothing but worry, and I'll do it alone.

I wish Esri would show up. I dare him to show up. I will scream at him. He tried to convince me that I had some power. But look at the way I'm treated by my family. They wouldn't tiptoe around me if I had power.

My nerves heat up. My temples tingle. My thoughts mock me again.

Shouldn't you be on your way to galavant around the Unseen? Maybe while your family deals with your seizing body here, you can build a sand castle in your dream world.

"Shut up!" I yell.

Footsteps race out of the kitchen towards the stairs. "Chance, are you OK?" Dad says from the bottom step. "What was that noise?" Thank goodness he didn't hear what I actually said. He would think I've started hallucinating.

"Nothing, nothing," I say. "I just stubbed my toe on the stairs. I'm fine. Just headed up to bed."

"Oh, thank goodness," he says. He looks at Mom, and their eyes gossip about me: *A stubbed toe? What else can go wrong?*

"Get some rest, bud," Dad says.

There it is. That's what my parents think of me. One small outburst, and they're ready to call an ambulance. I know they love me, and they're concerned. But am I really this pathetic?

I had originally planned on faking my parents out again. I was going to shut the door from the outside so I could eavesdrop on their conversation. I know they'll talk openly once I'm locked away. But now I'm too mad to care. I open my door and flop onto my bed. My head starts to simmer.

My fingertips numb a bit. The sensation creeps up my arms. Part of me wants to have a seizure. I deserve it. A few stars pop up here and there. I tap my pocket. The pill is there. It waits, like always, to take me out of this reality and relieve the world of my nuisance for a few days. I slide my right hand into my pocket. I fiddle the little tablet with my fingers. I run my index finger around its circumference.

Just take it. It will be better for everyone. You're a liability right now. If you love your family, you will take it.

I pull the pill out of my pocket and stare at it. Less than a half

113

hour ago, my mind summoned the courage to step onto an open gap in a bridge over a bottomless pit. I climbed dozens of feet up a melting ice tower and ran boldly into a collapsing marble edifice. Now I'm ready to take this tiny little pill that will leave my mind and body completely helpless.

"Reality," I say. I raise the pill. I open my mouth.

Without warning or reason, my left arm involuntarily snatches hold of my right wrist before the pill reaches my face. I feel my right arm flex as it tries to force the pill into my mouth. The left overpowers it. I'm somehow an uninvolved bystander watching my limbs battle each other. It all unfolds independently from my mind. Before I can really comprehend what's happening, both of my arms crash to my bed. I freeze in disbelief and fear.

What's going on? What's happened to my body? How am I fighting myself?

My mind races back through the last few days. I revisit conversations with Esri and trips to the Unseen. Did something happen in there that could cause this? Had Esri taken control of my arm? He said he didn't have any power in the Seen. But what other explanation can there be?

Wait. He told me I had to leave my thoughts and feelings from the Seen behind me when I go into the Unseen. Does that work in reverse as well? Is part of my mind, the one that's starting to gain strength in the Unseen, still there? Is it taking control of my body in the Seen?

I need answers. I need to talk to Esri. I jump out of bed and swing my door open. I start to bound down the stairs, but Mom's and Dad's voices stop me. They're downstairs talking. I forgot. Dad's probably telling Mom the truth now.

"Man," I whisper to myself. There's no way I can get around them and get outside without being noticed and probably sent back to bed. I sit on the top step to think. Maybe they'll stop and go to bed soon. It's starting to get late. They must be tired.

I stay dead silent. Their voices start to come in clearly.

"What did he say when he finally talked to you?" Mom asks Dad.

"He said he was concerned," Dad replies. "He said the situation in the conflict zone is not under control like they thought it was. He's starting to lose faith in Dr. Jacob's ability to get the job done quickly. Even if the procedures are successful, he doesn't think it will be in time to use Paul and the others overseas."

Dad stops talking. Mom doesn't respond.

"It was encouraging to hear that Paul shouldn't be headed to combat," Dad continues. "But it's scary to think there might be super soldier terrorists gaining a foothold in an area our country is supposed to control."

"Did he seem like he was telling the truth?" Mom asks.

"Yes. He seemed completely honest. It almost seemed like he was relieved to see me. Relieved to drop that formal, military face, the one he uses in press conferences and video chats. He fears the President is using this program as a tool. He thinks our being the first nation to try out this technology shows our continued leadership in the world. The whole *serving our* country thing is just a front for the President's political gain. At least, that's General Palmer's take. He's worried—very worried—for the safety of the children, our unpreparedness in the region, and the storyline that's being sold to the country and especially to families like us."

"What did he suggest you do?" Mom asks.

"He actually thinks I can help. But he said the timing isn't right yet. He's going to reach out in a week or so with more instructions. So I'm here, and I'm waiting."

"This doesn't make sense, Joseph," Mom says. "Why would he talk to you like that? Isn't that against...I don't know...isn't this classified or something?"

"I believe him, Maggie," Dad says.

Mom starts to cry. "I don't understand. I just don't understand. What are we supposed to do?"

I hear Dad's footsteps move towards her. "We're going to be OK, but we're going to have to fight for our boy. At least we have some information. The General is on our side. That's a good thing"

I'm not so sure.

I need answers. I need them now, before tomorrow's training session.

Chapter 13

How am I supposed to get to the treehouse? Mom and Dad aren't leaving the kitchen any time soon. I can't risk sneaking by them. If I get caught, that will bring extra attention to me. I can't afford extra attention. Not when I need time alone. For the moment, a trip to the Unseen seems out of the question.

I go to my room and fall back on my bed. I exaggerate an exhale. The ceiling fan spins above me. I try to track an individual blade with my eyes, but I can only keep up for a second or two before it turns to a whirling blur. It hurts my head, so I roll onto my side. I see the window.

I could climb out the window and down to the ground. It's risky, but it's only one story high. I could slide down the side of the house. Wait, what if my parents come in to check on me? They're extra stressed right now. They pay extra attention to me when they're stressed. I need to convince them that I'm in bed.

I pull the comforter back. I line up pillows on the fitted sheet. I throw the covers over them and hope it looks like a body in bed sleeping. I step back to evaluate my work. It's OK, but not convincing.

Maybe it will look better in the dark. I switch off the light. I can't see anything. I crack open the door to let some light in. My timing is perfect. I hear Mom and Dad climbing the stairs. I take a rushed step towards my bed, but it's too late. They've seen me.

"Chance, what are you doing, honey?" Mom asks.

"Oh. Um, I was just coming down to say goodnight."

"Oh, we thought you had fallen asleep a while ago," Mom says, no doubt noticing that I'm still wearing my clothes from earlier today rather than pajamas.

"Oh. Yeah, maybe. I mean...I must have fallen asleep without knowing it, and just woke up. Sorry, I'm a little confused." I avoid eye contact. I rub my eyes as if they aren't used to the light.

My parents stand in silence for a moment. Have I been caught?

"I think he's sleep walking, babe," Dad guesses incorrectly. But it's fortunate for me. "Chance, let's get you back to bed." He puts one hand on my back and uses the other to open the door to the dark room.

Please don't see the pillow body. Please don't see the pillow body. Please don't see the pillow body.

"Yeah, it's dark in here. He's been out cold," Dad whispers to Mom. He guides me to my bed and pulls back the covers. "Geez, he's got his pillows all over the place. Definitely sleep walking. He'll remember some strange dreams in the morning."

Dad puts me in bed. They both kiss me on the head and say their goodnights. They close the door quietly behind them. I let out a huge sigh of relief. Then I hold my breath and stay silent until I hear their bedroom door close down the hall.

When I know they can't hear me, I exhale and jump out of bed. I reconstruct my pillow body double. It should work for the rest of the night. There's little chance they'll come back to my room tonight.

Time for an escape plan.

I need something to climb down on. I look in my closet. No ladder. No rope. Nothing. In the movies, closets conveniently provide plenty of things for kids to tie to their bedposts and rapel out the window. No such luck for me.

I walk to the window and look at the distance to the ground. My best bet is to jump into the bushes. I *think* they'll cushion my landing. I open the window. I swing one leg out. With one leg inside, and the other dangling outside, I pause and close my eyes. The air is cool, which provides a little relief from the humid summer air. I hope it will calm my nerves. After a few seconds I open my eyes. I don't know if I'm much calmer, but it's time to move.

The drop can't be more than ten to fifteen feet. But it feels much higher. It's also dark. No one is around. I'm supposed to be in bed. It all makes this seem like a bad idea.

I preach to myself: "You just stepped into an open gap above a bottomless chasm. You can handle a one story fall into some bushes."

But that was in dreamland.

"It wasn't dreamland. It was reality. A different reality, but reality. Plus, that world might be connected to this one. We might need it to save this one, to save my brother. I don't know, but I'm going to find out."

Is it? Do you have any idea what you're talking about? You might break your leg. What's your reality going to be then? Surgery. A hospital stay. Bedroom confinement. Do you want that? Do your parents deserve that? What will you tell them? An Omnituen from another dimension told you to do it? Sounds like a great idea. You'll end up in a mental institution.

I want to yell at my mind to *shut up*, but I know I need to be quiet, so I muster my self-control. What good will screaming out an open window in the middle of the night do? None. It will do zero good.

I preach some more: "In any world, in any reality, it's thoughts that control actions. My thoughts have power."

Power until you break a leg.

"In fear, I have no control. Get control."

Control all you want. Stupid thoughts lead to stupid decisions.

"You need answers, and it's up to you to get them, Chance."

"In two, three, four. Out, two, three, four." I breathe, but not to calm down. I breathe for courage. For action.

"One, two, three," and I swing the other leg out the window. I turn my body around, belly facing the house. I grip the window ledge and lower my body as far as I can without letting go. I look down. There's no turning back now. I'm too weak to pull myself up. I feel my heart pump in my chest and my chest thump against the side of the house. My legs are closer to the ground now, but too high for comfort.

"Here we go."

I let go. A brief moment of silence puts the world on pause. All I can do is wait for a crash. The wait can't be more than a second, but it feels like an eternity. I start to wonder how long the fall will take when a combination of evergreen leaves and spiky, breaking boxwood branches sting me back to reality. I've stopped. I mentally scan my body. Nothing seems broken. Scrapes introduce themselves from head to toe, but I doubt anything needs medical attention. I start to climb out of the trampled bush. Getting out is harder than falling in was, but I manage eventually. When I get to my feet, I brush off my shirt and shorts. I glance back up at my window. The drop looks like it's only a fraction of the distance from the ground perspective.

How are you going to get back in the house?

"No time for that. I need answers."

I run to the treehouse and scale the ladder. Esri isn't there. I feared he wouldn't be but hoped he would. I pace around. I anxiously scratch my head. I punch the wall. I don't know how to contact him. He has always just been here.

"OK, OK, OK," I mumble. "Let's see. You work in thoughts.

You know my thoughts. You should know that I need you here. So...OK. Here I am."

I wish I could concentrate. I feel like I should be able to sit here and focus. Meditate. Do something that shows intense importance in the world of thoughts. But I can't. I'm exhausted. The training sessions. Dad's return with bad news. Covering up the bad news. Sneaking out of the house. I don't have much left. My shoulders slump. My knees weaken. I fall to the floor and close my eyes, void of ideas to get me in touch with Esri.

"Why can't I just use my ability in the Unseen to change things in the Seen?" I ask the empty treehouse.

A chuckle washes in from the tree branch.

I jump up. "Shhh. Shut up! You're going to wake up my parents."

Esri ignores me. He holds his stomach. He stumbles along the branch, his laughter tilting him off balance. He laughs some more, collects himself, and bumbles into the treehouse. He plops into the corner like a piece of laundry dropped on the floor.

"Oh my, Chance," he says, shaking his head. "If only you could use your abilities in the Unseen to affect the Seen?"

"Well, yeah. I needed to get in touch with you and didn't know how. I thought it would be helpful to be able to think and make you appear."

He squeezes above his eyes and looks away. No more laughter.

"What? Tell me. What's wrong with that? It's late and I need some answers from you. I can't wait until morning."

"Why do you think I've come to you, Chance? Do you think that I care about your ability to go into the Unseen and drum up a taco bar, cross a treacherous bridge, or live through a collapsing stadium?"

I stare at him, probably blankly.

"I'm here because I *know* your work in the Unseen directly impacts the Seen. It's your purpose. And it's my purpose to make you see that. This isn't some trick or toy for you to play with. Your gift—my teaching—" He stands up and paces around the short treehouse walls. He struggles to find words. "To undermine your potential or to downplay its ability to make a difference in this world denies the value of your very existence."

"Well—" I don't know what to say.

"No *well*. No *buts*. No confusion. You must believe this now. And you must move!"

"OK," I say.

"OK?" he responds. "Does that mean an end to the incessant questioning the Unseen?"

"I guess you heard all of that?" I ask.

"I hear what you need to know."

"OK, I get it. I'm in."

"Better late than never, I suppose."

"And by the way, was it you that stopped my arm?" I ask.

"Come again?"

"Nevermind. It's nothing." What was it that made my left arm stop the other from putting the pill in my mouth? "OK, let's get started," I change the subject. "Show me how to have an impact. Let's go. Fist up, or whatever."

"Chance, you haven't the energy. You need sleep."

"I don't care. My family is losing it. My Dad has figured out that something's not right. Paul is in trouble. I need to know how to help. I need to know how now. Let's go."

Esri takes a step back. He raises one eyebrow and looks me up and down. "Fair enough. Let's proceed, shall we?"

Our fists rise together. We cross over to the Unseen.

We arrive in the usual blackness, but this time seated. We sit face to face, Esri looking at me with calculating eyes. I prepare for a lecture.

"There's a mystery to this place. To a few, it reveals its secrets. Not for your sake, Chance. And not for mine. But for a grander purpose. For those who humbly accept that secret and dedicate their understanding to learning more and serving their purpose, more is revealed. And now, it's for you to learn how this place, this boundless place, connects to smaller realities. Those in the Seen. Do you follow?"

"Eh— well."

"From the Unseen, we can travel to anyone, anywhere in the Seen."

"OK. You should have started with that."

He treats my suggestion like a gnat and waves it off. "We *both* can check in on others. But *you*, you can connect with them. First, you must learn to see them. We'll call it *navigating.* I'll navigate to start, and you will come with me. Watch. Learn. And then, you try on your own. Understood?"

"OK, but how does it work?" I ask.

"Come." He puts his fist up like he does to get us to the Unseen. "Put your fist against mine, and we'll begin."

I do as he says. Colors swirl round his wristband. My eyes are drawn to it. It's the only color in an open landscape of black. As my eyes fix on the band, beams of light explode out of it, reaching about six feet to each of our sides. The light organizes itself and creates a tunnel around us. Now we sit in a lighted tunnel. It looks like a passageway carved through the dark Unseen. From the outside, I imagine it looks like what I've pictured a wormhole to look like in outer space. Esri and I, still seated, begin to move across the floor of the tunnel. We pick up speed. I can't see any destination, just lights everywhere. It's like driving through an underground tunnel encompassed in lasers. Outside the lighted burrow I can see that everything remains dark. Endlessly dark. Our single portal of transportation is the only sign of...anything. We're moving faster. I feel wind. It dries out my mouth. I can't tell if the tunnel races by us, or if we race through the tunnel. I guess it doesn't really matter. Esri sits with his eyes closed. The tunnel bends left. It bends right. The curves continue until an image appears at the tunnel's end. We slow down.

He opens his eyes. We both focus our attention on the image that slowly comes into focus as we approach the end. It's a city. New York City. It's Time Square. The tunnel end opens and blurs most of Times Square to our view. We can only see a few square meters of a sidewalk. On that sidewalk, a man appears. It's like we're watching him on TV, but we've somehow joined the picture. The typical Unseen abyss and the lighted tube that we used to cut through to this scene has vanished.

"This is…" Esri pauses. "We'll call him John."

"OK, who's John?" I ask.

"That's no matter. It doesn't concern your training. But know this: John is lonely. He's from another part of the country. He moved here for business, and he misses his home and friends."

"OK?" I'm confused. "So, he's lonely, and—" before I can finish a sentence, Esri closes his eyes again and the tunnel of streaming lights comes back to life. It blots out New York city and we are back surrounded by our wormhole transportation. We race somewhere else. A similar sensation takes over. Once again I can't tell which is moving, the tunnel or us. A few bends pass. Esri opens his eyes. Another scene comes into view.

We approach. The tunnel opens and invites us closer. A house appears. It comes into focus. We zoom in on a window and what lies inside. An elderly man lies with his eyes closed. He rests in his bed with a pained expression on his face.

"This man is sick. He's dying. I'd wager he won't wake up in the morning."

"OK." I don't like this. I don't know what we're doing. I don't want to see lonely and dying people. "What are we do—" He cuts me off again. Esri closes his eyes. The tunnel lights return. Presumably, we're off to another scene. I guess I'll find out what Esri is doing when he's ready to stop and explain.

The next scene that appears is a heavily secured industrial building. Armed guards stand on both sides of a gate, which is connected to a perimeter of barbed wire fencing. The building has few windows. It's massive. Smoke stacks spew exhaust into the surrounding atmosphere. It looks like a top secret bomb making facility from a spy movie.

The tunnel takes us to a particular entrance. On the other side of the door, a familiar person sits peacefully asleep in what looks like a reclined dentist's chair.

"Who is that? I know her from somewhere."

The tunnel zooms closer to the sleeping teenager's face. It's Jane Simmons. She's one of the students taken from our school.

"That's Jane!" I yell and turn to Esri. "What is she—"

"She's scared," Esri interrupts. "Jane is scared. I presume the others feel the same."

"Wait, what? What do you mean she's scared. And why don't we just check on the others. Paul's in there, right? Where is this place? Show him to me. Where is he?"

Esri turns and looks at me. The scene at the end of the tunnel disappears. The lights from the tunnel fade. Blackness returns. Esri and I sit staring at each other again surrounded by the darkness. "I can't," he says.

"What do you mean, Esri? Take us back. Take us back. I want to see Paul!"

"Chance, calm—"

"No, I'm not calming down! I came to help. You said you would teach me to help. I'm here. We're in the Unseen. I'm ready to help. Take me to Paul, now!"

"Chance." Esri pauses. He waits to make sure I won't interrupt him again. I'm too upset to talk anymore. "Look at me. Follow my lead. I'll show you how to get to Paul."

I catch my breath and respond, "OK, tell me what you need to tell me."

"What do you remember about John?" he asks.

"What are you talking about? Who is John?"

"The man in Times Square," Esri says.

"Oh, yeah. He was lonely."

"And what about the elderly man?"

"He was dying."

"Right, and what about Jane?"

"She's one of Paul's classmates. She runs track. She was taken on the bus with Paul. She—"

"Yes, but what did I specifically say of Jane?" Esri asks.

"Um. She was scared."

"Yes. What do these three have in common?"

I think for a few seconds. "They are suffering? They need help? I don't know, what?"

"Your answers aren't wrong. But, it misses a unity between them and with you. You are connected to each of them, Chance." He stops. He waits for me to respond. I don't. "Each is experiencing something that you know. Empathy. You can empathize with them. You know loneliness. You know fear. You, at your young age, have faced death, and fortunately escaped. The bond between disconnected beings is empathy. It's the span between the Seen and Unseen."

"So as long as I have felt what a person is feeling, I can navigate to that person in the Unseen?" I ask.

"It's not the sole method, but it's the best. Remember, the Unseen is a realm of thoughts. For two beings already here in the Unseen, we can connect by intentionally engaging each other. But, that intentionality isn't possible between those in the Seen and the Unseen. John, Jane, and the old man don't know we're here. It's only through empathy that they can communicate with us. Oddly enough, empathy is a stronger communication than words in any environment."

"OK. So Jane was scared, and you were able to find her by empathizing with her. Why can't you do the same with Paul?"

He turns away from me. He doesn't want to answer me.

"I don't know yet, Chance," he admits. Is he embarrassed? "At present, I can only guess. Perhaps I haven't tapped into the right emotion. Perhaps I simply don't understand the way he feels. But truth be told, I presume something within the Unseen is interfering with navigation to Paul and the others. Jane is the only one of the students who I've been able to navigate to. I believe she was the first one who felt a natural fear before some *thing* happened. I'm yet to determine what that *thing* is, but you're the best bet to discover it. You can empathize with Paul in countless ways. Not just fear. You know him. You share a life with him. Your brotherhood is a bond molded by empathy."

"Got it," I say. "So, let's go. What do I do? Close my eyes and think of an experience we had together?"

"Patience, Chance," Esri says. "I can't risk teaching you with Paul. Or with any of these children, for that matter. I haven't determined the interference. Accordingly, I cannot understand the risk.. You'll need to learn with others first."

I want to yell at him. There's always a "not yet" with him.

"Chance, patience."

"I'd tell you to stay out of my head, but I know that's not going to happen. Where do we start? Let me guess: we can't today. I need some rest."

Esri looks spooked. "Did you just read...? No." Esri squeezes his brow.

"Wait, am I going to be able to read your mind one day?"

"Get some rest, Chance."

"I am, aren't I? Just tell me. I'll tell you the truth, seriously. I didn't just read your mind. It was just a guess. But, really, am I?"

Esri stands up. He walks away from me. I try to chase after him through the Unseen.

"Esri," I say.

"Goodnight," he responds without turning around.

I must have blinked my eyes. The next thing I see is the treehouse floor. The next thing I feel is my heavy body pinned against that floor.

Chapter 14

"Leverage your entire history of thoughts and emotions," Esri reminds me as we restart training a few days later. I had been forced to stay away from the treehouse and the Unseen for a few days. After sneaking back in the house with a spare key hidden outside, I didn't want to push my luck with my parents. But Esri isn't skipping a beat. He's ready to get started and wants me navigating through the Unseen without his assistance. "You've much in common with most of mankind. It's only a matter of letting your guard down and meeting them where they are. Don't overlook laughter and happiness. They're often more accessible than painful memories."

"OK," I say. "That sounds better than reliving some...well... painful moments."

"Don't shy away from pain, though," says Esri. "There's power in struggle. Nevertheless, for now, start with more enjoyable emotions. What's a joyful experience for you, Chance?"

I know the answer. It seems too simple and ordinary of a memory to build a powerful empathetic connection between the Seen and

Unseen. I'm sure Esri has already read my mind and sees scenes of family movie nights flashing through my head. Instead of admitting he knows what I'm thinking, he looks intently at my face. He's studying me again. Maybe he sees something he isn't used to.

"Tell me about it, Chance. The more you describe, the more evocative your thoughts will be, and the more precise your navigation."

"Family movie night is what I look forward to more than anything," I explain. "It doesn't matter what's going on, how stressful the week has been, how sick I am, whatever. Those nights are safe and fun, and everything else just goes away. We cozy up in the den together, and we're all there for each other, enjoying each other's company. The movie doesn't even matter that much. It's just the fact that we're together. For a couple of hours, it feels like nothing can touch us. My parents don't seem worried about my health. Paul is there with us, not away winning soccer games or planning for the future. I mean, I'm glad Paul does so well, and I'm glad my parents take my health so seriously, but it seems like when we get together those nights, all of that goes away. And we're all just there for each other. Loving each other. It feels...right."

"I see, yes," Esri says. "Well done, Chance." I look to his face. He's turned from me. He examines the light tunnel that's begun to shine around us. It saddens me a little to understand that he isn't compelled by our family ritual. I want him to understand how special it is. He's more interested in my ability to pull up genuine thought and emotion. I guess if that's what makes the Unseen work; that makes sense. But I'm still disappointed. As I think about the disconnect between Esri's interest and my own, the colors of the tunnel change. They mute; the moving lines slow from a race to a steady flow.

Esri stops his examination and turns back to me, his mouth hanging open. He seems confused. "Don't stop, Chance. Keep thinking about your family and movie nights. If you keep changing your thoughts and emotional pattern, you won't build a connection strong enough to navigate to someone in the Seen. Family is a common, positive emotion. There are plenty of people to connect to out there. Carry on."

I draw my eyes away from Esri. I close them. I try to imagine one specific night. Paul's team had won the league championship earlier in the day. For the first time in months, the attention was off me and my health. Mom and Dad were proud of him, and I was too. We had gathered in our usual spot, and we missed at least the first half of the movie because we were too caught up talking about the game. Everyone wore genuine smiles. They had actually put my health out of their minds for a while, and they were happy. I was happy.

"Keep going," Esri directs.

I open one eye to see if the lights are coming back. They are. Esri walks around the tunnel and investigates the lights as if reading fine print. He puts his hand near the surface without touching.

I close my eyes again, squeezing them tight, and continue thinking. I fix my mind to dwell on that night. Buttery smells of popcorn waft through the air. Soft blankets and pillows pile on the couch. Movie scores play background music for our conversation. It's perfect.

When I open my eyes, the tunnel has fully encapsulated us. We're headed somewhere. Instead of arriving at a single scene, we slow at a fork in the tunnel.

"What's this?" I ask.

"Where would you like to go, Chance? It's your navigation."

I take a closer look at each tunnel. A blurry scene appears at the entrance of each option, both of them families. One shows a couple jointly holding a new, sleeping baby. Another shows a family in a foreign country. It looks like a family night, just like ours, but without the movie.

"Let's go there," I say gesturing to the family night.

"It's your navigation, Chance," Esri says. "I can't get us there."

"OK, but what do I do?"

"What's that family feeling, Chance? Can you see it? Can you feel it?"

I think more about that night with my family. I imagine it taking place in the house displayed before me. The more I focus, the closer we move. The fork falls away and we head down a single route towards the scene. The movement pauses. My view zooms so close to the scene, it feels like I'm there. A family of six gathers around a fire inside a shack of some sort. Just outside the door, I can see abandoned buildings and dirt streets littered with burning trash. Armed soldiers march along the streets. Inside the shack, which is built with walls of cardboard secured by string and tape, however, the family smiles. All of them. Much like the family movie night in my mind's eye, this family has managed to ignore the tragedy just outside their home. They've rid their minds of the devastation where they live, and are simply enjoying each other's company. I feel their peace among chaos. It's perfect.

The tunnel disappears. I sit with the family in their home. They don't see me, but continue their conversation. I can't understand the foreign language they're speaking, but I don't need to know the words to understand what they feel. Despite all that's wrong around them, this is right.

I smile. I could stare at this scene forever, but Esri interrupts: "Well done, Chance. Let's move on."

The light tunnel reappears while I sit in the room. The family and their home are blotted out. I'm traveling elsewhere, to my disappointment. The tunnel that removed me from that family disappears. It's back to the dark emptiness that I've become accustomed to in the Unseen.

Esri and I sit facing each other. "Any thoughts?" he asks.

"Good," I say. "I didn't want to leave."

"Yes, I know," he says.

"Let me guess," I say. "We have to keep going?"

"You aren't reading my mind, Chance," Esri snarks.

"Fine," I sat. "What's next?"

"Shall we try laughter? Can you think of a time when you belly laughed so hard that you couldn't stop. Maybe one of those times when you continued to laugh well after the event because the mere thought of it brought it all back."

I think for a few seconds. An involuntary smile overwhelms my face. Esri notices.

"Yes, that," he assures me.

Paul and I had our cousins spend a weekend with us. We always have fun together, but one night everyone was feeling especially silly. Dad took silliness to an entirely new level when he decided to show us that a fart could catch fire. We didn't believe him at the time, which only inspired him to prove us wrong.

He sat on the floor, rocked back and forth a few times, and threw his legs towards his face and then over his head. In a nearly upside down position, he lit a match and let out the squeakiest of noises from his backside. What he hadn't prepared for was the flammability of his pants. He wore flannel pajama bottoms, which are quite flammable. The expected small flame spread quickly down both pants legs, and Dad went from *man in vulnerable position* to *man on fire* in the time it took to pass a little gas.

At first, we were all terrified. Luckily, Mom had the thought to smother the fire with a quilt. She basically tackled him and the fire vanished quickly. Once we understood that Dad was unburned, we nearly died laughing. My oldest cousin had to rush to the bathroom and cackle over the toilet. Once he stopped laughing, we learned that he thought he was going to throw up because he was laughing so hard. For the remainder of the weekend and to this day, I instantly chuckle when recalling that scene.

The tunnel is back, full of racing colors. Esri stands by my side. We take off, faster than before. I notice another fork ahead. Scenes start to form at the entrance to each option. Before I can evaluate, though, a crackling noise interrupts. The streams of light that construct the tunnel flicker. The entire tunnel splutters. More crackling and buzzing noises echo through the air.

"Esri, what's going on?" I ask as I turn my head to him. His face looks concerned. He surveys the tunnel and Unseen surrounding it, 360 degrees.

He turns in slow circles, taking everything in. His calm but concerned voice instructs me: "Be still for a moment. Allow me to—" He doesn't finish his sentence.

We're still moving through a tunnel, but there's something filling the black outside it. Streaks of lightning punish the area around us. Then, the entire structure begins to break down. The sense of movement stops. As it does, the light tunnel is nothing more than disjointed, blinking lights. The lightning storm is now fully visible. My heart feels like it has moved to my throat. I hear my heartbeat in my ears. The tunnel vanishes completely. Eerie sounds accompany the lightning storm that we've found ourselves in.

That was a voice.

"Esri, was that someone else?" I ask.

"Shh," he cuts me off. "Silence." He continues to look up and around. His full attention surveys the Unseen world around us, a version I've never seen before.

What's going on? We need to get out of here.

"Esri, maybe we should—"

"Chance! Quiet," Esri commands. "Stand up. Come here." He motions for me to come close to him.

I pop up and move towards him. I tuck myself under his arm like a chick to a mother hen. As I do, a movement over our heads seizes our attention. Esri holds up his hand in the direction of the moving object. A beam of light projects from his palm to the mass. Esri's light reveals the first thing I've witnessed in the Unseen that hasn't been intentionally created by Esri or me. It isn't anything I recognize. It looks like a dense gray cloud tangled with remnants of black trash bags. It hovers in the air like tissue paper over an upward facing fan. It's in a constant state of changing shape. Esri holds up his other palm, and focuses a second beam of light at the object. When the light hits it, a screech echoes around us. It stings my eardrums. But the pain pales in comparison to the fear that grabs me.

"Stay still," Esri directs. The light from his palm changes to an intense green, and the beam narrows in diameter. The change causes the creature, I guess it's a creature, to let out an even more shrill scream. It begins to bounce around the area above us, like a bird trapped inside a room. The green light never loses contact.

The creature pings against imaginary walls around us. Esri's eyes narrow, and the screams increase in volume. The volume peaks and then the scream and the mass both start reducing. It continues to bounce around, never breaking free from Esri's control. It slows and continues to shrink until it's barely there.

Esri seems to have the situation under control. He divides his attention between me and the floating body.

"Join your fist to mine, like we do to get in here." He says. I do. The colors that usually make up the tunnel are captured in his wrist. "On the count of three, pull your fist away from mine as hard as you can." Seems easy enough. I prepare myself.

On the count of "one," it feels like our fists are instantly magnetized with opposite charges.

On "two" the magnetic force could lift a car off the ground. I ready myself to slam into him by the count of "three."

I don't remember hearing three.

The next thing I know, I'm lying on the floor of my treehouse. Soft afternoon sunlight filters through the leaves around us. Esri crouches over me.

"You OK?" he asks.

"Yeah, I think," I reply. "What was that thing?" I shake my head a little. My body feels like the typical post- Unseen lead weight, and my head pounds in pain. I can still hear that shrill scream.

"Just as you aren't alone here in the Seen, you aren't alone in the Unseen. The more you navigate, the more likely you are to run into others. As long as everybody in the Unseen is content with their own circumstances, no issues arise. With infinite space, there's no natural competition. However, when you see signs of an interruption like you saw this time, that means someone knows where you are. They want to interfere with you and your mission.

"Chance, your training must get faster. You learned to navigate quickly, but now you must learn to bridge before things get worse."

"Bridge?" I ask.

"Yes, communicate with those in the Seen from the Unseen. That's your purpose. Your power."

"OK. But what was that thing? And what does it want from me?"

"Try to forget that for now, Chance. For now, get rest. You'll learn to bridge first thing tomorrow. That will take all of you and more."

"Yeah, I get that, but shouldn't I know what's after me? Does this have something to do with Paul, or Dr. Jacbos, or something else? Is it another human, or an Omnituen? Or something else. Esri, be honest with me. I'm not going to be focused if I have to go into that training wondering what the heck is going on in there. What's going on?"

"Fair enough," he concedes. "You need some assurance. This requires explanation and some time."

I struggle to prop myself up on the treehouse wall as Esri watches, unable to physically interfere. I'm too exhausted to move farther on my own.

"I had much preferred to wait until you were fully trained to explain the full details of the Unseen and Omnituens. Nevertheless, that time has come...now."

"I guess things don't always go as planned, huh?" I ask rhetorically.

He grins. "If things seem to be going as planned, look out. You're missing something."

Chapter 15

"**O**mnituens are created, not born," Esri starts. "No school. No job. We're created in the Unseen and given a mission. We receive two pieces of information to guide us on our mission: our core strength and our core weakness. We rely on this information to make decisions. Carrying out a mission in an infinite world completely controlled by thought amounts to billions, maybe trillions of decisions. Understanding and accepting our core strengths and weaknesses helps us make sound decisions and avoid temptation and destruction."

"What's your mission? What are your characteristics? Wait, let me guess the weakness."

He holds up a hand. I stop talking.

"The collective role of Omnituens is to maintain the Unseen for its purpose within all of creation. Although the Unseen is separate from the Seen, it is designed to act in harmony with the Seen. The Unseen and Seen are separate but intertwined elements of creation.

"Because the Unseen is part of the same creation as the Seen, it won't surprise you that the Unseen is corruptible. Indeed, it has been corrupted. Not all Omnituens submit to their mission. They ignore their core weakness and abuse their core strength to suit their own mission. Any Omnituen who embarks on a mission that doesn't play a role in maintaining the Unseen for its purpose within all creation opposes it. Omnituens are either on-mission, or they are against it. There's no blend between the two. This is why we are all told of our core weakness, so we will be on guard."

"So, you guys are kind of like angels that keep the spiritual world working well, and every once in a while, an angel falls, decides to go his own way, and makes it harder on the rest of you?" I ask.

"If that helps you picture it, fine, but let me continue.

"What you saw was interference from an off-mission Omnituen. It has abandoned its original mission. Whatever its off-mission plans are, it took an interest in your navigation. Perhaps it wants to destroy you, use you, or something else. Regardless, it saw your navigation as an opportunity to corrupt you for its own purposes."

He pauses. He's noticed the confusion, maybe the horror, growing inside me.

I think: "That thing could have destroyed me? I thought I was just...thought. How could a thought destroy me?"

Esri looks down. He rubs his forehead. "This is why I didn't want to share until you were fully trained. Chance, as we've seen, thoughts are powerful. That Omnituen couldn't destroy your body in the Seen. But it could have completely controlled you in the Unseen. You're now connected in these two worlds. Everything you do, wherever you are, flows from your mind. A destroyed mind in the Unseen will undoubtedly end your body in the Seen."

"Connected?" I ask. "Wait! My arm. It was my thoughts that stopped the other arm from putting the pill in my mouth?"

Esri nods his head.

"Oh, man." My mind races. Gears turn. But, I struggle to wrap my mind around this news. Until now, I've managed to keep these two worlds separate. My fingers begin to tingle. My mouth waters. I tap my pocket. The pill is still there. How am I supposed to go in there and risk my mind being destroyed so that my parents find me dead in my treehouse? My head aches. I want to puke. I'm too tired to pace in agitation, but my thumbs are rubbing holes in my palms again.

"Chance, it's OK," Esri tries to calm me down. "This is why I've come: to help you. You can manage this. You're meant to manage this."

I'm not so sure.

"I'm not ready," I say. "I don't have enough training. I don't know how to deal with something like that!"

Esri lowers his eyes again. He mumbles to himself. He's trying to calm himself down now.

"I can't risk that, Esri. I need a plan. If something goes wrong, my parents need to know what's happened. I can't do this."

"Wait," Esri raises his voice, but remains calm.

"I can't," I say. "I'm sorry. I'm just...I'm just not ready. I can't go back in there for now. Can't we do some sort of training out here until I'm stronger? Can't we just—"

"My mission is to identify and train targets," he interrupts, ignoring my pushback. "Targets are the humans who can navigate both the Seen and Unseen. You, Chance, are a target. You are my mission. And no, I will not let you stay out here. Unless it turns out that you are not a target, and I am mistaken, you will come with me and train as others have trained with me over hundreds of human generations. Rarely have I been wrong about targets. I trust my core strength, which is discernment. Over generations of discerning targets, I've become matchlessly efficient. Hear me now, Chance Dawson: Stop hiding behind that blasted mask of weakness and incompetence that you've used to escape reality. Blot out the misguided "disabled" talk you've been poisoned with by those that don't understand your potential. Own your purpose!"

I've never seen him blow up like this. It startles me. I'm actually kind of thankful for it. It stopped the stress that was starting to build up. While I sit in fear of this crazy man standing in front of me, I finally stop thinking about me, my problems, my weakness, and my plans.

"Can I guess your weakness now? Craziness?"

He narrows his eyes. I can see another outburst growing in his chest. He restrains himself.

"OK, fine," I say. "No more of *that* talk. I'm still in. What do I need to know about these off-mission Omnituens?"

"Do you have the energy to come back in for a spell?" he asks. "I'll navigate. You'll be shielded from off-mission Omnituens. We'll locate others in the Unseen by navigation paths. It's possible that others could see that someone is with me, but they won't be able to identify who it is unless they take the time, power, and risk to break in."

"Yeah, I guess," I reply reluctantly. "If that's the best way to show me what's going on, let's head back in."

I'm not looking forward to this. I'm exhausted. I've agreed to go back into the Unseen, but I can't move to get started. I hold my arm out. Esri comes to me. We touch fists and flash back into the Unseen.

My mental fatigue clings to me, but it's not as bad as the physical exhaustion I had been feeling just a moment ago. We walk side by side through darkness. We walk towards nothing I recognize. No scenes appear. I look up to Esri. His eyes are closed. What is he searching for? Before I can ask a question, he stops.

He sticks out his fist and orders: "Now."

I push my fist against his, and the tunnels form more quickly than any navigation tunnel I've seen yet. We travel faster than I'm accustomed. Before I've adjusted to the travel speed, we come to an abrupt halt. If this had happened in the physical world, momentum would have made us crash straight through the scene that has popped up in front of us.

Esri holds his pointer finger in front of his lips. "Stay perfectly quiet. Duck behind that hill." He points to a small ridge in the scene in front of us. As we start towards the scene, the tunnel fades away. We're transplanted into a new world. This place makes the training ground city look like a child's creation. We crawl on our stomachs to the ridge of a small hill and look over it into a lush valley. The landscape leading to the bottom is painted with green grass and wildflowers. The warmth of the colors pulls me to them and invites me down the hill. And then there's the smell: the sweetness of honey and the calm of lavender. I feel Esri's hand on my back. He grabs my shirt.

"Don't, Chance. Keep still. It is tempting, I know. But rule yourself. Stay put."

I didn't realize that I've already crawled a few yards down the hill. This place had pulled me into it without my knowledge. I return to the ridge and look back down the valley. At the bottom of the valley sits the most powerful cityscape I've ever seen. The skyscrapers shoot above the hill where we lay and continue through the clouds above. Unwheeled cars hover silently around the city blocks. Parks break up blocks of city towers. These aren't the city parks from the Seen. They include stadiums that could hold tens of thousands and rushing rivers with magnificent waterfalls. A park visitor jumps from the top of one waterfall. My gut drops. I prepare my eyes to see him meet his crushing death. Instead, he enters the water gracefully and emerges from the water moments later. He walks to the shore, dries off, and hugs his smiling family.

At different points around the city, drones zoom down to cars and pedestrians. The drones make deliveries. Some deliver food. Others display a screen through which people talk to each other. When the conversation ends, the screen vanishes and the drone moves on.

I'm in awe.

"Inviting, no?" Esri asks.

"It's amazing! What is it?"

"It's the thought work of an off-mission Omnituen named...well, I won't say his name."

"Why not?" I ask.

"I've visited this place before. All of this is built to bring *him* glory. Those who you see down there, they're not people. They're either constructed purely of thought, or they're Omnituens that have sold their minds to him for permission to stay undisturbed in this place. There are monitors everywhere watching and listening. They endlessly capture what residents say about...*him*. If he hears talk that is contrary to his pride, he will destroy whomever said it. We'd rather those monitors not know we're here, so I won't say his name."

"They sell their minds to be here?"

"Yes."

"Why?"

"Remember the core weaknesses I mentioned?"

"Yeah," I say.

"There's only two: pride and impatience. Many Omnituens lose patience when their mission doesn't work out as planned or pieces of it take longer than expected. Since there is nothing physical here, there is no time. For me, I've trained human targets for many human generations. You can imagine that spending a great deal of time with a specific target only to have that target grow old and die before you can accomplish something is immensely frustrating. I'm not the only one with that mission. Others forget their bent towards impatience and would rather go mindless through a world like this where there is no tension to trigger impatience."

"It seems like an awesome place. Why wouldn't you want to spend your existence here?"

"It's mere vapor, Chance. Take a look. Look there. See that man by the east river?" He points down the valley where a river separates a meadow and the city.

"Observe him for a few minutes," Esri says.

I watch the man. A drone appears and delivers a sandwich. He eats the sandwich. Delight covers his face. He takes another fifteen steps or so. Another drone zooms in and delivers another sandwich. He scarfs the second sandwich just as quickly. I continue to look. The process repeats. Why isn't he full? Why doesn't he at least change up his order?

"The mouths of fools feed on folly."

"What?" I ask.

"He's mindless Chance. Nothing here is real." He crawls forward a few body lengths and picks a beautiful wildflower. He returns to my side and puts it close to my face for my examination. Esri rolls the stem back and forth between his thumb and index finger. The stem turns gray and starts to crumble. He continues to rub his fingers. The flower falls to pieces.

"In their impatience, they traded their minds for the hope of something better or easier. What they received was empty promises. They will never be satisfied here. No one would be."

"And what about the non-Omnituens down there?" I ask. "Are they robots or something? What are they doing here?"

"Ah," he says. "They cater to the second Omnituen core weakness, the weakness of the one who dreamed up this city."

Just then a loud, booming voice brings city life to a halt: "Residents of Nede, good afternoon. We hope you are having a wonderful day in our great city. It's time for our hourly acknowledgement and praise. One, two, three—"

An off-key orchestra of voices chants: "All hail, Zueck, the purest of Omnituen, for a mission accomplished by this fine city. Thanks be to him, and may he be eternally fruitful, and shall our minds serve him in all we do. Hail."

At the conclusion of the bizarre chorus, most go back to their fake activities. Six or seven drones appear from the corners of the city. They stop about thirty feet above the ground. Red lasers shoot from each. At the end of each laser, an Omnituen screams for a moment and then melts.

"What was that?" I ask.

"I guess they didn't join the hourly acknowledgement and praise," Esri says, quite matter of factly.

"Are you kidding me? Does this Zueck suffer from that same core weakness that I guess you do. You know, craziness?" I'm half kidding, but Esri's face tenses with fear.

"Chance, no! I told you not to—"

A drone flashes at the bottom of the hill. Two join its side. They rush up the hillside towards us.

"Fist. Now!" Esri yells. I punch his fist as hard as I can. I close my eyes. When I open them, I see my treehouse ceiling.

I take a few deep breaths. Breathing is the only movement I can manage. Exhaustion pins me to the floor.

"Sorry," I say.

"You should be," Esri agrees. He sits on the window ledge, his face solemn and distant.

"Won't happen again. I promise."

"Doesn't matter. We aren't going back. Get some rest." He changes the subject. He's clearly done with me for the day.

"By the way, what is the other Omnituen core weakness?" I ask.

"I already told you," he says as he walks away. "Pride." Before my eyes can catch up with him, he's gone.

Chapter 16

"What's next?" I ask Esri. I'm tired from the Unseen journey to Nede yesterday, but my body is starting to adjust to these trips. Day in and day out, I'm exhausted. But I can manage, and I'm ready to get on with it. I'm ready to find my brother.

"Bridging," Esri responds. "It's time to bridge."

I don't answer. I still don't really get what bridging is.

"You've learned to navigate. Your proficiency is...lacking, to say the least. Nonetheless, you *can* navigate, and we've little time to lose. Your brother—in fact, the entire Seen world—needs someone to connect through a bridge. You Chance, are the best option the world has."

His explanation doesn't give me any better clues about bridging, but it does make me feel completely inadequate. "Gee, thanks for the vote of confidence," I say, sarcastically. Encouragement isn't Esri's strong suit. I don't think he'd disagree if I asked him, but I don't think he cares, either. He knows his strength. He knows his weakness. And for now, he's picked me as his target, his mission.

Maybe it's good to know I'm mediocre at best.

"Humility comes before honor, Chance." He's read my mind again. He never responds to my sarcastic remark. Instead, he lifts his fist. I instinctively meet it with my own. We move to the Unseen as if switching worlds is as natural as getting out of bed in the morning.

We arrive to the usual blackness. There's nothing to see in any direction. The only difference between this trip and my very first trip to the Unseen is me. I'm used to it now. The endless dark that would—and should—terrify any normal human doesn't bother me anymore. I had hoped for a comfortable normalcy this summer. Instead, the Unseen and all its unsettling aspects have become my normal. For the moment, and just this moment, it's comforting.

"As you know, I cannot bridge," Esri starts. "No, that's left to humans...to you, for the moment. I'll navigate for now. Your inefficiency will disallow adequate time for bridging practice. Yes, I'll navigate to the nodes and then transfer intel to you. Shall we?"

"What?" I ask, completely confused. "Nodes? Intel?"

His fingers grab for the bridge of his nose. He chokes back frustration. He slowly exhales, and drops his hand to his side. He looks at me with the phoniest smile I've seen from him.

"Nodes are the individuals we navigate to. The individuals you will hopefully connect to. Intel is the collection of all information needed for a strong navigation and bridge. I've been navigating for generations. I'm extremely efficient at both reading intel and navigating to intended nodes. We'll leverage my ability to

navigate. I'll relay the information I gather to you. That will...
should grant you the best chance to bridge. To bridge, you need
be fully immersed into what the node feels and sees. The more
you know, the stronger connection you'll experience. When the
connection grows strong enough for communication between you
and the node, a bridge occurs. That bridge is what connects the
Unseen to the Seen. You will give the node eyes from the Unseen
to make decisions in the Seen."

"So, instead of you being like an angel, I'll be like an angel?"
I ask, half-joking.

"Don't flatter yourself, Chance," Esri rebukes. "You're no angel,
and neither am I. We both have a purpose. The more labels you
attach to your ability, the more likely you are to become consumed
with the label rather than your mission."

"OK, fine. Relax. I'm just trying to understand this without
getting overwhelmed. It's a lot." Esri had a sincere fear of falling
off-mission. After seeing what I saw in Nede, I guess it shouldn't
surprise me. "Alright, let's go I guess."

Esri raises a hand signaling I need to wait. I know when he
wants me to be patient. I oblige. He closes his eyes. I would've
thought he'd fallen into a peaceful mediation if it weren't for the
movement behind his eyelids. His eyes rapidly bounce back and
forth and up and down. Whatever's going on inside his head is
far from meditation. He's searching and searching and searching
faster. If he's evaluating *nodes*, as he calls them, or gathering *intel*,

he's making decisions at an unfathomable rate. It looks...unhuman.

Before I start to feel too uncomfortable, his eyes open. "Shall we begin? I've located a potential node." Our fists join. We move through a light tunnel typical of an Esri navigation. We arrive at the scene of a sleeping boy. He looks my age.

"He's dreaming," Esri explains. "You know this dream. You've dreamt it many times before. He's arrived at school. It's the last day of the semester. There are two tasks to accomplish before he goes on break. One, turn in a project that he's worked on the entire term. He's forgotten that project at home. And two—"

"He has a test, and he hasn't studied," I interrupt.

"Precisely," Esri says. He raises his fist again.

"What's that for?" I ask.

"Intel transfer," he says.

We join fists. I'm thrust into a dream. It's eerily similar to the one I've dreamt many times. The typical feelings flood through me: fear, embarrassment, uncertainty. I know this isn't my dream, but I feel an urge to solve the problem. How can I get a hold of the project? How can I get it delivered to school? How can I figure out everything on the test in the next few minutes? I hate this dream, but it's as familiar as the bed I sleep in every night.

"That's it," Esri encourages. "The connection is now strong. You should be able to bridge. Make a suggestion."

"Make a suggestion?" I ask.

"Yes. Help him solve his problem. You've been here before. You know the whole picture."

"Well, there's no good answers in the dream. He needs to wake up."

At my mention of waking up, the boy sits straight up. I can't see or feel his dream any more. The bridge, I guess the bridge, is gone.

"What happened?" I ask.

"All connection broke down when he woke up," Esri explains. "You could fully empathize with him in that dream. But now, he's somewhere else entirely. The second he woke up, his fears from the dream vanished. You see him now only because it's my navigation. If this were your navigation, you would have likely lost the node altogether."

"What?" I ask.

He starts to grab for his forehead, but stops himself. "Do you know what he's feeling right now?" Esri asks.

I look at the boy. He's gotten out of bed. He's getting a drink of water. I never get out of bed after a bad dream.

"Oh," I say. "No. I have no idea what he's doing or what he's feeling. I see what you mean. Was that OK, then? Did I do it correctly?"

"There's no *correct* way to bridge. You must find connection through common experience and grow that connection through continued questioning, listening, and understanding. It will take years to become proficient. For now, we'll hope to achieve a long enough bridge with Paul to get some information, or give him some direction. With that, you should be able to get him the help he needs."

"OK, so let's navigate to Paul," I say.

"Not yet," says Esri. "I've been unable to locate or understand the odd activity surrounding Paul and the other students with him. I feel it's related to the...encounter we experienced. If that off-mission Omnituen is waiting to intercept us, you won't have the strength to fight it off. We need you to practice more. You need to be able to bridge with someone else first, someone unguarded, while they're awake."

Maybe that makes sense. I don't know. Unlike Esri, I've never trained anyone to bridge two worlds before, but it aggravates me. Every time we make progress, Esri comes up with another reason to keep me from Paul. If the whole point of me *fulfilling my purpose* is to get Paul back, I want to get on with it. My face starts to burn.

"Chance, name something that you've done many, many times that evokes a strong emotion," Esri says, ignoring my frustration. I know the answer, but I'm not sure I want to feel those emotions. It's sitting in an exam room at my Neurologist's office. It might be the most accessible memory I have. The cold room and even colder examination table make it impossible to feel comfortable. The smell of disinfectant might kill germs, but it kills happiness too. The fluorescent lights make everything from the wallpaper to the patients look sick. I'm never there for good news, so the wait for the doctor, the wait for bad news, is long, longer than should be allowed. And dreadful. It's always dreadful. Nothing positive comes from trips to the doctor. If I'm there, my parents are worried, and their biggest worries are soon to be confirmed. I always try to mask my fear to help them, but that makes my stomach hurt. I always feel like a phony, a liar.

Playing this scene through my mind is enough for Esri to set us off towards a new node. I haven't said a word, but we're on our way.

In moments, a painful scene comes into focus. A boy my age sits on an examination table. I can see his bones through his skin. He wears a hospital gown that's too big for his underweight body. The slightest breeze will drag the gown off his body and his body off the table. He's bald. The awful lights make his skin appear a pale yellow. I hope it's the lights. His face is vacant. He stares at the hospital bracelet around his arm. It reads *Moses, Peter.*

Tears well up in my eyes. I want to jump into that room and give him a hug. Not because I have any answers for him. I don't even know what's wrong with him. But I know what he's feeling, and I want him to know that he's not alone.

Esri puts his hand on my shoulder. I cover his hand with mine. When our hands touch, I feel a surge in my temples. I haven't moved, but I'm somehow closer to the boy. I can smell the room. It reeks of disinfectant. The kind is different from my doctor's office, but it's definitely disinfectant. The fluorescent lights over his head buzz. The bench he sits on is hard. The padding has worn out, and it's freezing.

"What's happening, Esri?" I ask. "It feels like I'm in there with him, but I'm not."

Esri doesn't answer. I look back at the boy. He stays rigidly still. His eyes are the only part of his body that doesn't look paper light. His eyes are dark and heavy. They're something worse than scared. They're hopeless.

"What would you like him to know, Chance?" Esri asks.

"What I want to tell him doesn't matter," I reply.

"Why's that?"

"Because it might not be true," I reply. I feel a tear trickle down my face. "I don't know if it will get better. It might not. He doesn't believe it, and he's probably right."

"What does he need to know, then?" Esri asks.

"It might not get better, and that's OK!" I shout. "This is who you are, and that's OK!" I say to the boy. "You're here because you are supposed to be here. If you make it another year, or just another minute, you are here. And that is good, because that's who you are!"

I stop talking. I close my eyes. I can't take much more. It hurts. This whole place hurts. It might hurt worse than actual doctors' offices, post-seizure headaches, and losing my brother.

"Go on, Chance. That's right." Esri says. I know Esri wants to encourage me, but I don't care. I hate this feeling. I want it to stop. I don't want to *go on*. I want to stop.

"Have a look at his face, Chance."

"No, I want out of here," I say. "I can't do this. I hate it. I don't want to bridge if this is what it takes. I can't do this!"

"Understood, Chance. But—"

"You don't understand anything!" I shout. "You've said it yourself! You're just thoughts! You don't know what *that* feels like." I point at the boy. "You don't know what it feels like to sit there on one of those tables with your head pounding, choking back puke."

As I scream, the tunnel starts to blink. The Unseen world switches on and off between light tunnel and pitch black.

"Stop acting like you understand." I continue to scream at Esri, "You can't even die! And death, that's the only thing that boy in there can think of."

The black of the Unseen begins to break down. Flashes of the treehouse pop up around us. I continue screaming at Esri. I tell him all that's unfair with the world, and with him, and with everything he's asked me to do. The two worlds that confine me, the Seen and the Unseen, can't figure out where I belong. I yell, and Esri stares. One moment, we're in the treehouse. The next, we're back in the dark Unseen. Back and forth we go. The switching is as erratic as my fit.

I want out. I feel the pill in my pocket. I grab it.

I yell one more time at Esri: "Go away!" I collapse in a pile of weakness. I can't say anymore. I can't move. I lay with my eyes closed for who knows how long.

I breathe. No, my body breathes for me. If it were up to me, I would stop.

When I open my eyes, I'm in the treehouse. Esri stands over me. He stares down at me in silence. His eyes evaluate me unimpressed. He crouches down next to me.

"Go on inside," he says, like nothing unusual has happened. "Rest. It's time to rescue your family."

"Family?" I ask. Doesn't he mean Paul? I sit up. "What do you mean, family?" I look around. He's gone.

Chapter 17

I've learned to effectively ignore the physical effects of the Unseen on my Seen body, but the emotional toll of yesterday's trip is new. Before Esri taught me to bridge, I had started to understand and appreciate the power of the Unseen. Understanding that power had started to excite me. I was ready to fully commit. But if an effective bridge means drumming up my own painful past, that's a commitment level I hadn't anticipated. Can I make a regular practice of reliving my worst days again and again?

I'm not so sure.

And, I still don't understand how I can help. Does it do any good to say to a sick child, "I know how bad you feel, and I'm sorry"?

I'm not so sure.

I avoid the treehouse. I need a break from the Unseen and its demands. I don't want to see Esri. I know his perspective, and I know he isn't willing to see things from mine. I don't need another explanation. I don't want to see him bat away imaginary flies out of frustration with my questions and hesitations. I need some space to think on my own.

I roll out of bed later than usual. I sloth towards my bedroom door. I open it and start towards the stairs. Before I descend, a door slams. It reverberates throughout the house. A family photo on the wall in front of me shudders. It comes to rest unlevel, the left corner slouching lower than the right.

What's going on?

I move downstairs with caution. I brace myself for anger from someone. Whoever shut that door is mad. But as I reach the bottom step, the house is impossibly silent. I peek my head into the den. No one. I tiptoe to the kitchen. As I approach, I hear a kitchen chair shift the slightest amount. I pause and inhale. I hold my breath, fearful for what I'll find upon entry.

I hate that I feel the need to do this. The kitchen has always been a joyful refuge full of tasty food and good conversations, an escape from the stressful world outside the walls of our house. But now, it's become a townhall for bad news. The best news that's come out of this kitchen since Paul left is something along the lines of *it's not as bad as we thought*.

I can't hold my breath any longer. I exhale and creep into the kitchen. Mom sits at her usual spot. Her face is masked by that absent look that she hasn't been able to escape since Paul left. She doesn't budge when I enter. She holds a piece of paper in her hand. An opened envelope rests on the table in front of her.

"Hey, Mom," I try to ease her out of her daze and into a conversation. "Did we get another letter from Paul?"

Mom rotates her head towards me. Our eyes connect. She doesn't need to say anything. It's more bad news. I walk to her and slip the paper from her fingers. It's a letter, but it isn't from Paul.

Dear Families,

We regret to inform you of two situations that will require an extension of the Project Delta timeline and the delayed return of your children. First, the therapy is taking longer than we originally anticipated. Our results have all been positive, but the actual procedures involved are more involved than we originally expected. Accordingly, your children remain under medical supervision, with many still undergoing active therapy. Once all children have completed therapy and adequately recovered in a controlled post-op environment, we will allow the children to contact you. We expect this to be another few weeks. We will keep you informed.

Secondly, the situation in the conflict region has not yet been resolved. The US and its allies have been unable to recover some of the key assets and are now engaged in military conflict with terrorist cells. Some of the cells do appear to be using the "Super Soldier" techniques we anticipated. Accordingly, and out of an abundance of caution, some of the program participants will be moved to a US military base in the area as soon as they are stable. Our plan and goal in the area remains the same. We do not anticipate active combat for any participants, but are moving selected participants out of precaution. In the event that we are forced to deploy project participants into active combat, the decision will need to be made quickly, resulting in prompt action. We will do our best to keep families informed.

Finally, the President will address the nation in the coming days with details on the project and the conflict. He will share less details than this letter. We felt it appropriate to prepare you for this press conference before the President addresses the nation as a whole.

We appreciate your cooperation, understanding, and patience.

Sincerely,
General Davis Palmer

I look back to Mom. "Did Dad leave to try and find him?" I ask.

Mom nods her head. Tears well in her eyes. She cups her mouth with one hand. It's not enough. She buries her face in both hands, and the tears flow unrestricted. I wrap my arms around her. I'm no good at this. I need Dad.

"Dad will figure something out," I try to assure her. I'm sure my tone isn't convincing. After all, I don't believe my own words.

I doubt any of our abilities to do anything, but I don't think my tone matters. She isn't listening to me. She's in a different world. Maybe she's in a world trying to find Paul. I don't know. I don't know much of anything.

"He'll figure it out," I say. "Stay positive. We'll get him back. We'll sit tight and see what the President has to say soon."

My gut draws me to the treehouse. I'm not ready to go back in, but I'm not sure I have a choice. Until now, something in the back of my mind has continued to tell me that everything will be OK with or without my help in the Unseen. Maybe it would be Dad finding Paul. Maybe it would be an end to the conflict overseas. Maybe the project would just finish, and Paul would come back. I don't know, but that thought has stuck with me throughout the past few weeks. But now, things are worse than ever. There doesn't seem to be a good option in the Seen. I wish I knew where Dad was going, and if he'd been able to connect with General Palmer. Had they discussed meeting again, or is Dad just trying to track him down?

I know how I can find my Dad, but I don't want to admit it. I don't want to go to the Unseen. I don't want to *need* it. I don't want to need Esri. I sigh. My ticket to finding Dad isn't in this world. It's in the Unseen. One more trip, and I'll have some answers. I don't really know what happens when I find him though. Would it actually help?

I'm not so sure.

I leave the house. I need to get out. For the first time in a while, I don't leave by the back door. Instead, I walk out the front door and start walking down the street. The summer heat radiates off the asphalt. I try to block the swarming thoughts that are overwhelming my head, but they're relentless. The endless stream of worries mixed with the choking humidity feels suffocating.

You shouldn't get too far away from home. Mom will worry, and she's already worried enough. She'll think you've had an episode.

"Shut up," I say quietly but sternly. "I'm fine." I pat my pocket. It's there, waiting.

You'll need to take the pill soon. Things are about to get bad. Dad is gone. Paul's not coming back. You'll make things worse if you are stressed out. You can help your family if you are at home asleep. Stay out of the way.

I walk faster. I pull at my shirt collar. It's so hot. It's hard to breathe. But for some reason, I can't control the urge to run. Can I run away from my own thoughts? No. Who am I fooling? Thoughts are the one thing I'll never get away from. Seen or Unseen, my thoughts will never leave me alone.

"Just, stop!" I snap. "I need some room. Just let me figure this out, and I'll be fine. I don't need the pill, and I don't need to go to sleep. I need to help, I just have to figure out how to do it."

In home. In bed. That's how you can help. The doctors say it. Your parents say it. Even Paul wants you to stay calm. You can't stay calm out here. You'll lose it, Chance. You'll lose it.

I jam my hand into my pocket. I feel the pill. The sweat from my fingers turns the pill's surface instantly chalky. If I mess with it much more, it will start to break down.

Better take it before it disintegrates. You don't want to get stuck out here without medicine. You'll wake up in a hospital and then be shipped to an institution. Get home, Chance.

I release the pill into my pants pocket. I pace in circles in the middle of the street. I grab at my hair in frustration. I'm running out of breath. I move to the side of the street and sit on the curb.

What should I do? I take a few deep breaths. I close my eyes. I try to imagine where Dad's gone off to. I urge my brain to recall the military base where I'd seen Jane. Paul must be there too.

Is Dad meeting General Palmer? Is Paul strapped to a chair like Jane was? I fear he is. I know he is. I just haven't seen it yet.

"Sitting here thinking about it isn't going to help," I tell myself. "There's only one way to find out."

I jump to my feet and rush towards home. I ignore the heat and my exhaustion. I sprint. I come to the front porch, jump the stairs, and fling the door open. I run straight through the house and out the backdoor. I climb the ladder and look for Esri. He's not there.

"Come on!" I yell. "I'm here. Let's go. I'm ready to help my family! That's what you said to do right? Help my family? Well, let's go."

He doesn't show. I crawl onto the window sill where he often waits. I walk out onto the branch where I've seen him effortlessly balance so many times. I ignore the height and walk further and further away from the treehouse.

Mom's voice startles me. "Chance! What are you doing? You'll hurt yourself."

My balance falters and I crouch on the branch, grasping the limb. Mom is standing on the step to the back door, ready to spring toward me in case I look like I'm falling.

"Mom," I answer, shakily. "You scared me." I had completely forgotten she might notice me through the kitchen window. I collect myself and steady my voice. I notice how far from the ground I am. My stomach lurches.

"I'm fine, Mom," I lie. "Just thought I'd see what it was like out here. Paul used to do it."

"Well, get down, please," she orders. "You'll give me a heart attack."

I shimmy along the branch and climb back into the treehouse. She watches me all the way. Once inside, I poke my head out. "See, I'm good. Nothing to worry about." I force a smile to reassure her. My heart beats a million times a minute.

"Don't do that again, Chance. We can't afford any accidents right now."

"OK, Mom. Sorry. I'll just hang out here for a while." Mom waves. She goes back inside and closes the door.

I exhale in relief. Crisis averted. "If that idiot would have just been here when I needed him, that wouldn't—"

"What idiot is that?" Esri interrupts.

I jump, startled again. "Geez. Do you have to do that? I've got enough on my mind right now. I don't need you adding to it."

"Fair enough," he says. He stares at me, his dark eyes glittering as he sizes me up. He strokes his chin. "It sounds as if you need assistance, no?"

"Really?" I ask, sarcastically. I want to punch him.

"Well, go on. Make that fist. But, let's forgo the punch; just place it right—"

I wind up and punch him straight in the first that he's held up. If he were just another person, it would have hurt; it would have hurt badly. But he's not. Instead of bracing for the pain of bones breaking, I open my eyes to an empty, endlessly black canvas.

Chapter 18

"Your father," Esri starts. "Shall we find him?"

"Yeah. I mean, unless he's already headed back home. I don't know where he went. Do you know? Because, in just a few days—"

"Let tomorrow worry about itself, Chance," Esri cuts me off. "I need you, and your father needs you here right now."

"OK. Let's go. What do I do?"

"I'll navigate. You'll bridge. Put yourself in your father's shoes. Where is he going? Why? What is he feeling right now, Chance?"

"Umm...I don't....He's worried. But also mad. And he's determined. Dad is always determined, no matter what he's feeling."

"And how do you know he's mad? What was he doing when you last saw him. Bring the scene to your mind."

"I didn't see him. I just heard him. And felt him. He slammed the door so hard I thought the house would collapse."

"Yes. Well done, Chance. Go on."

"That's all I know," I say. "He just...left. The door spoke his anger for him. I didn't hear him say a word. Then when I saw my mom in the kitchen, that confirmed something was wrong. Dad had left. He was going after Paul. He's scared. He's mad. I'm sure he feels helpless. But he has to try something. He always has to try to fix problems. It doesn't matter if he can or not. He has to try."

"I see. Put your fist to mine. Keep thinking about your father," Esri says. "I'll find him. Hopefully you'll be ready to bridge when we locate him."

I touch Esri's fist with mine. I close my eyes. Colors flash through my closed eyelids. I try to ignore them and concentrate on Dad. I imagine the look on his face. I think back to those doctors' visits full of nothing but bad news.

"There's nothing more we can do," they'd say. "We've tried all the medicines out there."

Dad never accepted those explanations. He'd pace around the room and grab at his head: "If you can't come up with something, somebody else can. Who else can we talk to?" he'd ask.

He must feel the same way now. There's no way he's satisfied with the limited information we have about Paul. But at the same time, the whole situation is out of his control. His oldest son is at the mercy of a decorated military General and a brilliant scientist who've been given free reign to run experiments on kids. It's the helplessness that's grating on him. Sure, he wants Paul safe. He wants our family back together. But the fact that he can't do anything about it, that's the dagger stabbing him to the core.

"We've arrived, Chance," Esri interrupts my thoughts.

I open my eyes. The end of the tunnel shows my father driving. His fierce gaze is fixed on the road in front of him. Esri and I stand and watch him.

"Where's he going?" I ask.

"Soon," Esri responds. "You'll see soon. He's almost there."

Dad pulls the car into a parking lot. The lot is empty except for one nondescript vehicle. Dad parks his car next to the other. He kills the engine. He jumps out like a lion pouncing on prey. The driver of the other car opens his door slowly, methodically. The driver barely gets a leg out of the door before Dad is on him.

"What's going on, General?" Dad yells. "I want answers. I want them now! Where's my son? I want to see my son."

General Palmer calmly continues to exit his car like Dad isn't even there. As he stands, his shoulder nudges Dad backwards. Once standing, the General holds up a defensive hand; it grazes Dad's puffed up chest. The General's stoic face starkly contrasts Dad's hysteria.

"I understand," General Palmer starts. "There have been some issues that have kept me from contacting you sooner."

"Issues?" Dad raises his voice further. "What kind of issues?"

The General looks down at the ground. He drops the stone soldier face and kicks some dirt. "Well...I actually need your assistance with that. So please, calm down a moment so I can explain."

At the mention of assistance, Dad relaxes. His shoulders fall naturally. His jaw unclenches. General Palmer is handling Dad perfectly. He's coming up with something for Dad *to do*. He's going to give Dad the opportunity to *fix* something. Dad eases off attack mode. He looks ready to help.

"OK, fine. Good. Tell me what's going on. Let's get started."

"It's Dr. Jacobs," the General starts. "He's not... He's not who I thought he was. He's got the participants, er, the kids in a medical facility, and they're under...well they're safe, but they're under... They are all kind of in a comatose state."

"What?" Dad's face melts in horror. "Can't you get to them? Let's break them out!"

"Yes, I know where they are, and Jacobs doesn't suspect I think something's wrong."

"OK. Good. So let's sneak into this facility and break them out. Come on, you've got the whole military at your back. Surely you can handle one mad scientist. What are we waiting for?"

General Palmer looks at the ground again. He turns from Dad and kicks a piece of gravel. He purses his lips like he's getting ready to blow a bubble. He exhales forcefully.

"General, talk to me," Dad says.

"It's the President," General Palmer says. "It's worse than I thought."

"Chance," Esri interrupts my watching. "You need to get in there. It's time to bridge."

"What do I do? What do I do?"

"You know your father. What's he going to say? How's he going to react? Go there, Chance. Go there in your mind. Do it now!"

I fix my eyes on Dad's face. I try to imagine his pain, his fear, his anger, his shock. It's all there. I know it. Thoughts spin through my head. I feel my Unseen self pulling towards the vision of my father in front of me. I feel close to him, family movie night close.

The bridge starts like it did with the boy in the hospital room. I prepare myself to communicate with Dad, but my thoughts start to spin out of control. My head feels like a top that's started to lose speed. I can't keep balance. My entire self, the Unseen version, starts to unravel and tilt back and forth. The scene of Dad and General Palmer pushes away from Esri and me.

"Get control, Chance," Esri says. "Your father wants information. He needs information to help. How does he get people to talk, Chance. How does he do it?"

I fight to stay with Dad. What's going on? Why can't I keep the bridge?

I grit my teeth. I try to focus on Dad until Esri yells: "Chance! Get out!"

"What?" I scream. "Get out of what?"

I lose the connection with Dad. The scene has vanished. We're back in black emptiness. I hear screeching in the distance, but I see nothing.

"Chance, you must leave the Unseen. We've been found. I must attend to it."

"What? Who found us? What are they going to do? Where are you going?"

"I don't know yet, but you need to stay away. I'll take care of it. Go back to the treehouse. Stay there until I return. Do not stay in the Unseen! You will not make it out alive."

"I don't understand, Esri."

"You don't need to understand. You need to listen and do what I tell you to do. Go! Now!"

Esri turns from me. He moves towards the screeching. He's either forgotten that I don't know how to leave the Unseen on my own, or he doesn't have time to transfer me out. Not knowing what else to do, I pull myself into a defensive position and crouch like a child taking cover from a monster in the closet.

Esri doesn't move far before the sound's source reveals itself. Dark gray swarms of smoky clouds fill the space in front of me. Within minutes, the clouds blot out the normal darkness around me so my field of vision is only ten or twenty feet. Then the clouds split down the middle, and a rush of wind gushes towards Esri from the divide. The force is directed at Esri, but even I feel blown particles of something pepper my eyes. I throw up my arms against the force and struggle to watch what's happening. The wind sweeps through Esri, tearing at his clothes and threatening to knock him over. I prepare for Esri to be swept away. He leans into the gale to keep his feet. He's about to falter. Just before he succumbs, the wind dies. The dust and the fog that had been mucking up the view instantly clear. A man stands about twenty paces in front of Esri.

The man doesn't look too different from Esri. They would be about the same age if Esri had one, and they're both roughly the same size and build. He's clothed from head to toe in black. Like Esri, he wears an oversized knit cap that flops behind his head. He must be an Omnituen. Esri's back is to me, so I can't tell if he recognizes the newcomer.

Faster than I can blink, the man reaches for his right pocket as if he were drawing a pistol in a gun battle. In matched speed, Esri braces himself with one foot in front of the other and both arms crossed in front of his face.

Nothing happens. The man doesn't throw or shoot anything. There was nothing for Esri to actually block.

The man relaxes and starts to laugh. "Oh Esri, you never cease to bring a smile to my face with your endless worry. If I wanted to end you, wouldn't I have just snuck up on you and your little friend?"

Esri relaxes his shielding stance. He stands upright, calm but guarded.

"How can I help you, Scab?" Esri questions with mock pleasantness.

"Don't play games with me, Esri. You know what I want. Stay out of this project."

"And what project is this?"

"Oh, do shut up. Do you really want to sacrifice a human in an outmatched attempt to stop the rightful next step in the evolution of the Seen world? We've been stuck with this useless lot for generations. Aren't you bored with them? It's time to move on, and you know it. Your little boy can't do anything to stop it, but you sure will get him killed telling him he can. You know that, Esri. Be honest. Step back and let nature...well, a new nature, take reign over the Seen. It's time."

"Your evil is as fresh as spring water, Scab," Esri responds. "I have my mission. I will see it through."

"Even if you have to sacrifice a human life? Really, I'm shocked," Scab scoffs sarcastically. "I didn't take you to be so cold-hearted."

"You've had your say, Scab. Anything else?"

"I just don't want to see anyone hurt, Esri. Especially in vain. He can't even navigate on his own, let alone bridge. There's no stopping a force this strong with so little power, don't you think? But there is little doubt he'll die in trying."

Esri doesn't reply. My heart sinks into my stomach. Has Esri been lying to me about my ability? Is he leading me to my own demise? Why? Am I being used?

"Well, I'll leave you to him," Scab continues. "He's still here by the way. You really should teach him to get out of here on his own. But I digress. Until later, Esri. Hopefully not soon."

Puffs of smoke rise from the ground, and charcoal clouds fall from above. They consume Scab. He leaves much the way he came. The news that I am still in the Unseen seems to catch Esri off guard. He turns quickly. Our eyes meet. He rushes to me.

"What are you doing here?" he asks. "I told you to—"

"I don't know how," I interrupt.

"Right," he concedes with a sigh. Discouragement ravages his body. He slowly lifts his fist before me. He won't look me in the eye. I tap my fist to his, and our arms fall to our sides.

I blink. We're both back in the treehouse, me, exhausted; Esri, dejected.

We sit in silence for a few moments. Esri searches for the right words to say. I break the silence.

"Scab?" I ask.

"An off-mission Omnituen," Esri answers.

"I figured," I say. "Esri, is there any truth to what he said?"

His eyes meet mine for the first time since we left the Unseen.

"Chance, I can *see* most things in your world, but I *know* very little for certain. However, I know Scab is off- mission and determined to bring others off-mission as well through lies and deceit. I know my mission, and I know my strengths. I also know your innate potential. We train to realize that potential. We hope that when the time comes for you to act, you're ready."

My head aches at his explanation. I wish he would've just said *no*. I don't know how to respond. I'm certainly not assured that I'm ready. I suspect we're running out of time to prepare, though, and I'll have to try whether I'm ready or not.

Chapter 19

Esri vanishes and leaves me alone to drag my exhausted self to the house. Pinks and oranges paint the summer sky above the roofline. For a moment, I take in the view. My family loves summer skies. Together we love them. I ignore the reality of my summer break, full of uncertainty as it is, and instead I let peace wash over me. It cools my nerves. I can't clear my mind completely; without Mom and Dad...and Paul, so the peace doesn't last long. I drop my eyes from the sky to the house. I catch motion in the kitchen window.

Mom paces back and forth, her phone glued to her ear. Who is she talking to? Is it Dad? She flings her hands back and forth erratically. She always talks with her hands, but this looks unhinged. Whoever she's talking to has her riled.

I pull up energy I didn't know I had to run to the door, but I stop short of crashing in. I want to listen to her conversation. If she knows I'm within earshot, she'll downplay whatever it is that's going on. I need the truth, not to be kept from it.

I grab the doorknob and let out a deep sigh to steady my breathing after my short run. I slowly turn the knob counterclockwise and gently apply pressure to budge the door open. With a slight pop, the door gives way. I squint my eyes and place my ear to the door crack, hoping I have been quiet enough.

She keeps talking. I don't think she heard the door or me. She's talking a mile a minute. I hear her continued pacing. The speed of her words makes it seem like she's under a time limit.

"But what does that mean, Joseph? Are you actually going with him to the base or wherever they are keeping Paul?"

While Mom waits for an answer, I slowly push the door further open. I slip my body inside and push the door shut as silently as possible. I put my back against the wall that separates the back entry from the kitchen. I slide closer to the kitchen entryway. A chair squeaks against the floor. I hear her body drop into it. Her nervous fingers tap on the table.

I quiet my breathing as much as possible. I wait for her next words.

"I know he's being helpful, but I don't understand how you think the two of you can waltz into some top security military base and break a bunch of kids out. And—"

She stops before completing her sentence. Dad must have cut her off.

"But you don't know that, Joseph! He's told you he thinks the President is *in on it*. Don't you think they've probably added more guards and guns and whatever? I mean, the General who was leading this thing left! He's with you! Don't you think that has caused some reactions?"

Her tapping fingers switch to pounding fists. She starts to talk a few more times. Each time, Dad cuts her off. Dad's made up his mind. He has a plan. That's clear. I wonder how far into that plan he's already waded. Is he at the base? Is he on his way?

My aching body is beginning to protest holding so still pressed against the wall.

"Joseph, please just promise me....just promise me…". She isn't cut off this time. She's just at a loss for words. What do you say to a man with no military experience who is about to enter a top secret military facility and disrupt a project that has been announced to the entire world as the single most important program to the future of the country?

The conversation is coming to its natural end. There's nothing left to say. I slide back towards the backdoor.

"Just be careful. I can't lose you too." Silence looms thick for five or six heavy seconds. "I love you too."

I open the backdoor and then close it to announce my entry. "Mom," I shout. "Hey, where are you?"

"I'm in the kitchen, honey." I hear a beep as she ends the call with my dad.

I enter the kitchen and find her sitting at the table. She picks at her fingers. She looks nervous, but it's an improvement from the blank stare that's so often seized her face.

"What's going on?" I ask.

"I spoke to your father, Chance."

"Great, is he coming home? Did he learn anything?"

"He's not coming home yet, but he did learn some things. He thinks, anyway."

"OK, so where's he going? Does he know where Paul is, or when he's getting out?" I play dumb, hoping she'll be honest with me. She hesitates.

"He's going with General Palmer to the military base where Paul and the others are being held." She pauses and looks at me. She wants to continue but doesn't know if she should. She doesn't want to frighten me or make me nervous. She bites her lip.

"It's OK, Mom. I'm fine. You can tell me. I'm not going to have an episode."

"General Palmer says that the program isn't going as expected. He says that they don't think they can actually perform the whole, you know, self-directed stuff— therapy, or whatever it's called." She buries her face in her hands, trying to protect me from her emotions as she fights back tears.

"So what is Dad going to do? Is he helping General Palmer or something?"

I force the appearance of patience while I wait for her to collect herself. I need to know more than *where* Dad is going. I need to know *what* he is doing if I'm going to navigate to him.

She manages to collect herself with a heavy exhale. "He and General Palmer are going to try to get Paul and the others out.

General Palmer says he knows how to do it without being caught."

"But if he's in charge of the program, why doesn't he just get the rest of the military to do it? Why doesn't he just tell the President? Is Dr. Jacobs holding them hostage or something like that?"

Mom doesn't answer right away. She shifts her eyes from me to the window and then around the room. She bounces her leg under the table and picks her fingernails some more.

"Sit down, Chance," Mom says. I know where this is going, but she doesn't know that I know. She's going to tell me. I appreciate that much, but she's going to tread lightly.

"Do you have your pill, Chance?"

"I'm fine, Mom. Just tell me." I snapped more than I should have. My tone pushes her back in her seat. She crosses her arms. She purses her lips. I can almost hear the debate in her head struggling with how much to share.

"I'm sorry. Yes, I have it. I just—I want to know what's going on."

"I know, hon. Hopefully, it will all be over soon." She pauses again. I choke back my anxiousness and fake patience. "General Palmer told your father that the President is covering it up. He says that the problems in the conflict area are made up, and this was just a political stunt. Apparently there really were some experiments to be done, but the kids were never meant to be sent to an actual military conflict area. The General said it was stated this way to the American people so he could get permission to run the experiments and then look like a hero when he kept all of the kids out of harm's way. It was all to make him look good. So your Dad doesn't think there's any actual danger, but I'm still nervous."

"I don't know what to say," and that is true. Does Esri know any of this? Is it actually true?

"Me neither, Chance. I just want Paul and your father back home. I want us to have the summer we all dreamed of." She reaches out and touches my face. "The summer that you had talked about."

"Me too, Mom." We sit and look at each other. What would Mom say if she knew I was about to warp into some other dimension and try to spy on what Dad and Paul are actually up to?

"What now?" I ask.

"The President is making another news announcement in—" she looks down at her watch. "Oh, in just a few minutes, actually. The General says it will all be lies, but we might as well watch."

"Yeah, let's go watch."

We walk together to the den. Mom picks up the remote and finds the channel. A still screen reads: *Stay tuned for a special announcement from the President of the United States of America.*

We wait in silence. Mom, expecting she knows the truth, is prepared to ignore the President's message and wait patiently for Dad to contact us. She sits down on the couch and holds her arm over the back, expecting me to slide in next to her. I have too much nervous energy. I can hardly stand still. I shift in my shoes waiting to hear what the President has to say so I can get back to the Unseen and see what's *really* going on.

Time drags. The message on the screen mocks my impatience. Eventually, the screen flashes to an empty podium. The President enters the screen from a distance— not too dissimilar from a scene coming into focus in the Unseen. Strange.

"Good evening,

"Not long ago, I addressed this nation with news unprecedented in our history. I informed Amercians that we had implemented a draft of sorts where a small group of young and willing Americans had agreed to come under US military authority to participate in a groundbreaking program involving self-directed evolutionary techniques. We started the program due to a present conflict that threatens our nation on the other side of the planet. Tonight, I stand in front of you to update you on the program and on that threat.

"First, I'm happy to report that the technical side of the program is going well. Each participant is healthy, encouraged to serve their country, and ready for the necessary action. Dr. Jacobs and General Palmer could not be more pleased with their progress and the success of these revolutionary techniques. Additionally, the participants have remained in touch with their families and the families have had direct conversations with both General Palmer and Dr. Jacobs.

"Unfortunately, the situation in the conflict area has not eased as we had hoped. While we are not ready to go to war or increase force, we have decided to move the program participants to a secure military base in the conflict area. We will continue to use diplomatic and traditional techniques to resolve the matter. We are moving the program participants to the area out of an abundance of caution.

"In the event that we are forced to deploy the program participants, that decision would be made under considerable time constraints. Accordingly, preparations are already underway to move program participants to the aforementioned military locations. We ask that you continue to keep these participants in your thoughts and prayers, as well as the US military, General Palmer, and Dr. Jacobs. Thank you for your attention and continued support.

"Good night."

Mom points the remote at the TV and turns it off.

"Well, General Palmer wasn't kidding was he?" Mom says. "How can he stand up there and lie so easily to an entire nation? The nation that elected him."

I want to bolt towards the treehouse. I know I can't. Not this late. Not while Mom wants to talk. She will want me to rest, especially after the news she just dropped. I look at her. She's about to tell me to go to bed.

"Well, better get some rest, hon," she says, as predicted. I want to argue, and I start to. But I catch myself.

"Yeah, guess so." I can always sneak back out my window.

"Here, I'll walk you up," she says. "That's alright. I'll manage."

"Nah. I'd be happy to. After all, what else am I going to do? Your father's obviously not around, and if I stay down here, I'll just worry. Let's go."

"You've got to be kidding me," I think to myself. "Of all nights."

We walk up the stairs together. Mom tries changing the subject a couple different times, but she can't keep her mind off Dad and Paul and the President and everything. Her thoughts and comments keep wandering back into worry, and then she changes the subject again. I get myself ready for bed in my bathroom. She sits on my bed and continues chattering while I brush me teeth and wash my face, mentioning everything from "You want to go see that movie?" to "What are you thinking about for colleges? Do you think you'll want to follow Paul?" Each attempted distraction ends with a return to the only thing on our minds: Paul and Dad.

I just want her to leave. I want to get back to the treehouse, back to the Unseen. I have work to do. As I leave the bathroom, I notice she's fallen silent. The situation has gone from bad to worse: she's already laid down on my bed and fallen fast asleep.

"Oh, no," I think.

I look at the clock. It's late. I could use the rest. My next trip to the Unseen will be the most intense yet. That's for sure. Right now I'm still wiped out from my last trip. I crawl under my covers and tuck an extra blanket around Mom.

I concede that I'm not heading to the Unseen without a good night's sleep. I'll go first thing tomorrow morning. I just hope it won't be too late.

Chapter 20

I wake earlier than normal. The sky shows its waking colors, but the sun won't break the horizon for another thirty or forty minutes. I roll my head to the side. Mom is sound asleep beside me. Apparently she slept through the night instead and never made it to her own room.

I need to get to the treehouse, but I can't disturb her.

I slip out of bed. She rolls over and lets out a meager groan. How am I supposed to leave the house before sunrise and not have her freak out when she realizes I'm gone? I slip over to my dresser and grab a change of clothes. I quickly get ready in the bathroom, hoping she'll be awake when I'm finished. She's still sound asleep when I open the bathroom door though.

"You're just going to the treehouse," I think to myself. "not going after Dad or doing something crazy. You're not even leaving the yard. Right? Just tell her."

I walk around to Mom's side of the bed. I rest my hand on her shoulder. I give the slightest nudge. I whisper: "Mom." She doesn't budge.

"Mom," I say, a little louder.

She rolls away from me to the other side of the bed. The sound of my voice registered in her head, but it didn't pull her out of sleep. I walk back to the other side of the bed. I have no choice but to wake her up and let her know I'm going out.

But when I see her face, I change plans. Peace covers the features I've grown used to seeing in various stages of anxiety over the past few weeks. I can't upset that. She needs that. After all she's been through, she deserves some peace, even if she isn't awake to enjoy it.

I tear a scrap of paper off one of my old school notebooks and write a note. I go for informal and hopefully nonalarming:

Mom,
Didn't want to wake you. I woke up early. Going to the treehouse. See you in a bit.

Chance

I tape the note to the inside of my bedroom door. She can't miss it. I creep out of the room and close the door as quietly as possible. When it finally pulls closed, I exhale a breath I've been holding while preparing my escape in silence. Then I'm off. Down the stairs. Out the door. Up the treehouse ladder. I have things to see, navigations to make.

I pull myself through the hole in the treehouse floor and get to my feet. I look around. Esri isn't here. I look out the window. The branch is empty. This has happened before. He'll eventually show up. Eventually isn't good enough today though. I need to get into the Unseen now. No, actually, I needed to get in there yesterday before Dad left with General Palmer. I can't wait for Esri to show up on his terms. I don't need to be taught a lesson about patience. I don't want a lecture about my ability and how to use it. I need to get in there. I need to get in there now.

"OK, you've got this," I try to assure myself.

Got what?

"Oh, shut up," I say aloud. "I know what it's like to have a seizure. I know it's that same energy that can get me into the Unseen. I've done this tons now. I just need to do it. I will do it."

Fine. Do it. I'd like to see you try.

"OK." I clench my fists. I close my eyes. I squeeze them tight to concentrate. But I don't know what to concentrate on. No thoughts come. Nothing happens. I only feel a little embarrassed.

Right. You've got this. You don't belong in that world, Chance. It's dangerous, and you don't know anything about it. Esri basically said it himself when he didn't refute Scab's comments. You'll DIE trying to bridge to anything. Scab said it, and Esri didn't deny it. Go back home, Chance.

It doesn't make much sense to go in there alone. I don't know what I'm doing. Esri has hinted on multiple occasions that I might not be ready yet. But it doesn't matter. Life never happens as planned and rarely as you want. Paul wasn't prepared to go off to battle, but he volunteered when the opportunity, or supposed opportunity, called. Dad isn't trained to infiltrate top secret military facilities. But he is doing it because his son is trapped in one. My path to serving my family is in the Unseen. Prepared or not, I must go.

Don't be surprised when you fail. What are you going to do when you do fail? How hard will that be on your family? They've tried so hard to protect you. That pill in your pocket, that's your family looking after you at all times. Even when they are away or asleep.

I pat my pocket. Out of habit, I automatically transferred the tablet to my fresh clothes this morning. It's there.

"No," I yell. Muscles throughout my entire body tense. I squeeze my fists. I dig my toes into the insoles of my shoes. "There's no backing out now. They need me, and they need me now."

The blood that fuels my tensing muscles heats up. My temples burn. Stars start popping through the treehouse. The walls shift colors. My mouth waters. My anger bends towards fear, and I start to lose control. It doesn't feel like the organized entry I've come to know with Esri's help. It feels like an oncoming episode. Like collapsing at the dinner table. Like falling down the stairs at school. Like people asking me if I'm OK in muffled voices. Like I need to take the pill.

I pat the outside of my pocket. It's there, ready to take me back to safety. I slide my hand to the top of the pocket then slip my fingers in to touch the pill. It's chalky. It starts to disintegrate at the touch of my sweaty hands.

My nerves are on fire. I'm going to vomit.

Take it now! It's not too late.

I grasp the pill and yank it out of my pocket. I open my hand and stare at it. My breathing is short and rushed. I pant like a dog in summer heat. In all the confusion that has entered my life in the last few weeks, the decision before me now is simple. Take the pill and go back to safety or throw it away and risk everything to save my family.

I take one last look at the pill, close my fingers around it, make a fist, and throw what's left of the little powderly disc out the window.

My blood boils. My nerves burn through my skin. The ringing in my ears feels like it will ruin my eardrums. I blink uncontrollably.

When I open my eyes, I sit winded in the deep, dark nothingness of the Unseen.

Without Esri here to guide me, I sit alone and exposed.

"Where are you?" I ask nobody. My words echo throughout the void that surrounds me. My voice fades and then disappears. I sit in silence until a thundering rumble grows in the distance. I bring myself to my feet and walk towards the sound. A strike of red lightning flashes. I continue towards it. Is it Esri? What is he doing?

The sound intensifies and grows into something more organized than thunder. The lightning strikes aren't lightning from a storm but rather some intentional energy passing between two objects, neither of which I can see. In my desire to identify the source, I instinctively start running.

I arrive at a duel scene. Scab stands to the left, Esri to the right. Neither acknowledges my arrival. Each omnituen stares intently at the other. Neither makes a move, nor a sound. They stand like two mountain rams considering another attack in head-to-head combat.

What are they doing? Are they reading each other's minds? Is this some sort of mind chess game? I look at Esri. A calm concentration cloaks him from head to toe. I don't know what he's doing, but I don't feel scared as long as I keep my eyes on him. I try to avoid looking back at Scab, but I can't help myself. A hidden force draws my eyes away from Esri.

I glance at Scab. His dark eyes morph into a blood red. An evil smirk grows across his face. My heart thumps harder. Drips of red fluid leak from his eye sockets. Streams of the same violent liquid stream out of his shirt sleeves, down his palms, and drip off his fingers. The bitter taste of iron fills my mouth. I freeze. I can't remember why I'm here or how I got here. I hope only for rescue from this horror.

Before I can attempt to calm myself or beg Esri's help, Scab lifts his arms, the rivers of streaming scarlet liquid rising with them. The fluid rushes towards Esri like a horizontal waterfall. I can feel the heat coming off the flows. Esri doesn't flinch. Instead, his body disappears, and instantly reappears out of the flow path. Scab redirects the river from his hands in another direction. Again

Esri dodges. The process continues, each time Esri moving out of the way just in time to miss the flood.

The streams fade away. Scab pulls his arms back to his sides. He bends his elbows at a ninety degree angle. He rotates his wrists, and his palms facing upward. He extends his fingers, and yellow bolts of electricity explode from his hands into the sky. He closes his fists around the bolts, and thrusts his closed hands behind his head in a windup position. With an explosive step forward and an opening of his hands, Scab unleashes the current towards Esri. My stomach heaves, and I feel and taste bile in my mouth.

I look to investigate the damage Esri has suffered. But instead of damage, a translucent orb has formed around Esri's body. The force field deflects the current away from Esri. He seems unfazed, but I feel a piercing sensation in my own chest.

Scab closes his fists and returns to a standing position. The two resume their mind battle. I feel more out of place in this scene than anywhere, Seen or Unseen. A grimace crosses Esri's face. A muffled moan slips through his lips. Reflexively, I reach for him and scream: "Esri!"

Both Omnituens break their stare and turn in my direction.

"Chance," Esri says in a strained voice. "Your family. Go." He puts out his hand in my direction as an indicator to stop moving towards him, and to do what I'm told.

Scab laughs. "Oh, Esri. Do you think your little friend can help you in here?" He grabs his belly. He mockingly falls to his back and rolls around laughing.

"Your house, Scab, whatever it is—" I've never seen Esri struggle to speak like this. "It will fall."

Esri, crouching in pain, thrusts his fist in front of him. Blue streaks fire from his fist in Scab's direction. In an instant, Scab returns to his feet with a nonchalant hand open in front of him. He seems to catch the beam and calmly closes his fingers around it. He squeezes his now- formed fist. His hand shakes, and his eyes glow red. He winds up again and pitches Esri's blue streak back towards Esri. The protective shield returns around Esri, and Scab's counter is blocked.

Esri and Scab fix their gazes onto each other. The destructive forces exchanged between the two seem harmless compared to the invisible mental war between them.

Without breaking his concentration on Scab, Esri points his hand in my direction. He signals again for me to go.

"Right," I say. "My family."

I turn from a battle I can't possibly comprehend. I focus my thoughts on Dad. I think about Mom's conversation with him, his helping General Palmer, the President's cover up, and his leaving in anger and desperation.

As I focus on Dad's struggle, the navigation tunnel forms around me. I concentrate harder on Dad, his love for my family, and his desire to protect us at all costs. The tunnel thrusts me forward. I'm on my way. In moments, a scene comes into focus and my progress slows.

I see Dad and General Palmer approaching a massive facility. It's basically a walled fortress teeming with guards, protective fences, and armor. They walk towards a single door where two armed guards await them. General Palmer shows his ID badge and points to my Dad with some explanation. I can't hear the conversation quite yet, so I focus on Dad's face. What is he feeling? He looks poised but concerned.

The scene zooms closer to Dad and the General. The door in front of them opens. They enter the building. The halls are barren. Other than periodic doors, the building appears to be nothing more than concrete walls and flickering fluorescent lights.

General Palmer slows at a door on the left. He scans his ID badge beside the door and it clicks open. General Palmer gestures for Dad to enter first. Dad obliges. The two enter the room, which is completely dark. The door closes behind them. I can't see anything. I doubt they can either.

"Dad?" I scream.

The lights come on. Five armed guards stand in front of Dad with guns pointed directly at his face.

"Don't move! " one of them yells. "Let me see your hands!"

What's going on? "Dad!" I yell again.

"Woah, wait a minute," Dad reacts. He puts his hands up, compliantly. "What's going on?" He turns to General Palmer. "General, what's this?"

General Palmer ignores his question and turns for the door.

"Dad!" I scream. He doesn't hear me. "What's happening? General Palmer, help him. Help him!" I pound my fists against the air, but nothing happens. I collapse on the floor of the light tunnel, and the beaming lights dim.

"General!" Dad yells.

"What did you think?" General Palmer asks Dad as he approaches the door. The General shakes his head at Dad in disapproval. "Take him away." He motions for the guards to grab Dad, and they do. They walk him into a barred cell on the opposite side of the room. General Palmer disappears.

"Dad," I mumble. "Dad."

The dimmed tunnel lights flicker. The beams break and eventually scatter. My head spins. I grab the sides of my scalp and try to ease some of the dizziness. The black of the Unseen blows out from under me like leaves caught in a fall breeze. I close my eyes. When I open them, I'm on the treehouse floor.

I catch my breath and look around for Esri. He isn't there.

"Esri!" I yell. He doesn't respond. He doesn't come. Of course he doesn't come. I don't know why I expect him to. For all I know, he's still battling Scab for who knows what.

I look towards the house and see Mom through the kitchen window. She paces back and forth. I climb down the treehouse ladder and walk across the yard and to the backdoor. I shake off the Unseen grogginess and enter.

"Mom? Are you OK?" I don't know what time it is. The sun is up, but I don't know how long I've been in the Unseen.

"I'm in the kitchen, honey."

I enter the kitchen. Our eyes meet. Fear grips her face.

"What's wrong, Mom?"

"He was supposed to call. He was supposed to call this morning."

"And he hasn't?" I ask.

"He said if he hadn't called by ten, then......He said, if he hadn't called by ten, then—"

"What time is it Mom?"

She doesn't answer. I look at the clock on the wall. 12:30.

Chapter 21

I walk out of the kitchen and towards the backdoor. If this were any other day, I would stick around and try to comfort Mom. I would wait for an opportune time to slip back outside and into the treehouse. But not this day. Today I need to be elsewhere, and I need to be there now.

"Chance, where are you going?" Mom asks.

"Treehouse." I offer no explanation. I don't wait for the follow up question.

I burst through the backdoor. I march across the lawn. I scale the ladder. I don't look for Esri. He doesn't matter. His words matter though, and bits of his many lectures rush through my head:

You call it a disability. I call it access.

It's your gift; the gift that will allow you to be who you were meant to be.

I come to help you realize that those episodes, as you call them, are not something that you need cured.

I tell you the truth when I say there's power in your...what did you call it disability.

Stop hiding behind that blasted mask of weakness and incompetence that you've used to escape reality.

My mouth begins to water as his guidance replays itself in my mind's eye. Stars fill the treehouse until the walls can no longer contain them. I prepare for the treehouse to explode. Instead, stars pour out the window and form a path along the branch where Esri often sits. I follow the path.

My nerves warm, but it doesn't hurt. The stars, the color change, the heat, it all comforts me as I journey towards the Unseen. Any anxiousness or fear that I previously felt when switching to the Unseen flees my body. A single thought captures my mind: *this is where I'm supposed to be.*

I enter the Unseen alone. And today, it's OK. It's more than OK. I'm here with a purpose. It's time to get my family back. Although it's dark all around me, I don't feel like a stranger in a foreign land. I feel like I exist as part of the Unseen. I am part of it, and it is part of me.

I don't open my mouth, but I hear my voice call: "Paul." The volume is gentle, but it reverberates throughout the endless space around me. I wait for a response. Instead of a verbal acknowledgement, I feel Paul catch my call. My words hit his heart, and that connection pulls me to him.

The colored tunnel surrounds me. It carries me to my brother. It doesn't matter where he is. If he's in the military base with Dad or on a deserted island, it doesn't matter. I'm heading towards Paul, and nothing can stop that now. Of this, I'm sure.

As I travel, my attention on Paul intensifies. He was tricked into volunteering to serve. He risked his own life willingly. He was brave. And he stayed calm and positive for me. He wanted to make sure that I stayed positive and stress free. He loves me. Now it's time for me to return that care.

A scene gathers at the end of the tunnel. I see Paul reclining in a chair like the one Jane was sitting in when I saw her. Dozens of cords attach to his head and lead to countless monitors around the room where he sits. My body physically revolts at the sight of my unconscious brother. Knifing pain pierces my stomach. High pitched ringing stings my ears. My heart races. Blood rushes to my head.

"Paul!" I yell. He doesn't move. "Paul!" Nothing.

"What am I supposed to do?" I ask the Unseen. "I'm here. I've found him. I'm here. Paul, wake up! Wake up!"

A hand grasps my shoulder and distracts me from my panic. I turn and see Esri's face.

"Chance," he says. "Well done."

"Esri, there he is. He's in that chair, just like Jane. We have to get him out. What do—"

"No, not *we*, Chance," he says "*You* will get him out."

"What do you mean?" I ask. "I've said his name. I've navigated here. He isn't moving. I've told him to wake up. Tell me what to do."

"Chance, how did you get here?" he asks calmly.

"What?" I ask, confused. "Why are you asking that? We're here. Now I need to bridge. How do I bridge? Let's do it. Dad's in a cell, and Paul's...he's....well, he's right there. Wherever that is, in whatever that thing is."

"Answer the question, Chance."

"I don't know. I just thought about Paul and how he...he's brave, and he loves me, and he sacrificed for all of us, and then he got tricked." I pause. I continue: "And how I need to get him back. I'm supposed to get him back."

Esri smiles. He glances down at my arm. My eyes follow, and I notice a band of colored light encircling my wrist.

"It's your gate, Chance," Esri says. "You've navigated with my gate, but my gate can't bridge. Yours can. It is your gift, and now that you've accepted your responsibility to use it, it has made itself accessible. You've found your brother. Now go rescue him."

I keep my eyes fixed on the gate. Greens and blues and purples swirl. Without speaking, I hear my voice call Paul's name again. It originates deep in my chest. I feel it migrate down my arm towards my wrist. The gate swallows my unspoken words and then the circle breaks open. A path of light bridges the tunnel from where Esri and I stand to the scene where Paul is lying unconscious. I follow the bridge. In less than a moment, I stand in a room with Paul.

I see the others as well. They all sit in similar chairs hooked up to equipment. Each reclines completely still and unmoved by my presence. They weren't brought here to become American heroes.

They were brought here to be lab rats.

Am I really here?

"No," I hear Esri's voice say, but he isn't with me in the room. "You aren't physically there, but your thoughts have bridged with your brother, which is the most powerful connection in the universe."

I look around the room. The walls are similar to the halls that I saw Dad walk through with General Palmer. It's certainly the same facility. The room contains one door. I walk towards it and look through the small rectangular window. I see an armed guard on the other side of the reinforced glass.

"Chance," I hear Esri's voice. "Paul."

I move back to Paul. I put my hand on his chest. There's a weird sensation of touching him without actually touching him. The gate on my wrist glows. I feel my voice brew in my chest.

"Wake up, Paul," my voice resonates throughout the room.

Paul's eyes open. I jump back, startled.

Paul blinks his eyes a few times. He fights through grogginess. He looks down at his wrists and sees IVs stuck in both his forearms. A look of surprise shoots across his face. His hands spring to his head. His fingers examine the many cords attached to his head.

Surprise evolves into shock.

He looks around the room and sees his unconscious classmates surrounding him.

Shock escalates to horror.

He grabs his chest. He touches his head. He feels his bare legs. He wears only a hospital gown.

I don't know what to say, but I hear Esri's voice: "Calm him down, Chance."

"What? How?" My voice trembles. Tears well in my eyes.

"How did you get here, Chance?" Esri asks.

"Right. Paul. I'm here for Paul. My family. For love." I look at Paul. Of course, he can't hear my voice.

I feel more words growing in my heart. Before I can move, I hear my voice call: "Paul, it's Chance. You're going to be OK. I'm here to help you." My voice fills the room, startling Paul.

He turns in circles looking for the source of my voice, still clearly upset. He crashes against a metal table holding medical equipment. Syringes and scalpels crash to the floor.

"Chance, you must listen to me, and listen carefully," Esri's voice calls. "Paul must shut down the equipment, wake up his classmates, and get them out of this place."

"OK," I say.

I look at Paul. He sits on the floor, shaking. His eyes bounce around the room, trying to make sense of where he is and what he's seeing.

Esri continues: "On the wall across from the door, a keypad grants access to the machinery in this room. The code is 0423. He needs to enter that code and then hit *Disable* to safely bring the others out of their sleep state."

I try to put myself in Paul's position: scared, confused, and exposed. I close my eyes. My chest pounds. I hear a louder version of my voice fill the room: "Paul, wake the others up. Go to the keypad on the wall across from the door. Push 0423 and then *Disable*."

Paul balks at the sound again. He slides his body backwards across the narrow floor and stops when he is pressed against the wall opposite the door. He looks around the room some more. Again he finds no source for my voice. His eyes fix on the door. Then he looks up at the key panel above his right shoulder.

"Good," I hear my voice comfort him.

Paul rises to his feet. He looks at the key panel. He turns and surveys his classmates. He looks back to the key panel and considers the instruction.

Another voice blares through a loudspeaker: "Alert. Lab Room K. Subject 6 disconnected. Alert. Lab Room K. Subject 6 disconnected. Alert. Lab Room K. Subject 6 disconnected." The announcement continues. Paul turns and glances at the window set in the one door. I do the same.

The armed guard's face appears briefly and then vanishes. He shouts something down the hall.

"Chance, there's no time," Esri's voice yells over the relentless Lab Room K alert. "A secret door next to the panel will lead Paul and his classmates away from the room. General Palmer's soldiers will be on their way soon. Paul needs to push 0423 *Disable* to wake them up and then 0423 *Abort* to open the door. Now!"

"Paul! It's Chance. Listen to me now. You are in trouble. You've got to get everyone out. Hit 0423 *Disable* to wake everybody up and then 0423 *Abort* to open a secret door next to the panel."

Paul's eyes narrow. This time he doesn't hesitate. He turns back to the panel and enters the first code. Instantly, the others begin blinking their eyes through the grogginess that Paul has now completely shed.

They don't have time to examine their connected bodies in peace. The alert continues to blare through the sound system.

They start to panic, but Paul interrupts them: "Guys! We're in trouble. Follow me. There's a door this way." Paul punches in the code, and a section of the wall next to the panel slides open. It reveals a long tunnel in front of them.

"They must go, Chance," Esri shouts. My voice booms: "Go, now!"

"Come on, come on, come on!" Paul commands. "I'll explain later. Just trust me." The students leave their chairs. Chords yank from machinery. Monitors tip over. Medical equipment scatters across the room as the students scramble to the opening. Paul stays in the entryway until every one else has safely entered the tunnel.

The sound of marching fills the hall outside the room. My mind flashes back to the last day of school when marching boots stormed those halls. I wonder if Paul's did the same.

Paul's classmates are now in the tunnel, but Paul doesn't follow them. What is he doing?

"What are you doing?" I ask. He doesn't hear me.

Paul runs towards the main door where armed guards are about to burst in. He presses a button next to the door labeled *Lock*. He tests the handle. It hasn't locked. He looks up. A face appears in the window. It's General Palmer.

Paul rapidly enters the 0423 code and then pushes the *Lock* button again. A small *click* verifies success.

General Palmer yanks on the handle trying to open the door. He fails. His eyes meet Paul's through the protected glass. General Palmer scowls. Paul smirks then turns and flees towards the tunnel where his classmates wait for him.

General Palmer pounds on the door. "Dawson, open this door. Paul Dawson!" He pounds more and kicks at the door handle. He turns and yells down the hallway: "What's the override code for this? Jacobs, where are you?"

"Nice," I say to myself.

Paul enters the code on the wall panel and then hits the *Close* button. He slips into the tunnel just as the wall slides back into place. Paul and the students are out...for the moment.

Chapter 22

"Paul, what's going on?" someone asks as the students gather in the tunnel.

I watch them from the Unseen. I turn to Esri. He's watching another scene in another tunnel. I don't want to interrupt his focus.

"We're in trouble," Paul explains. Confusion distorts his face. He won't be able to hide it from the others. He needs an explanation quickly. He needs some direction too. "Just give me a minute, I'll—"

"We know we're in trouble, Paul," another student interrupts. "We've been in trouble since we got here. Where are we now? Do you know a way out of here?"

"How did you find that door, Paul?" another asks. "How did you wake up?"

I must do something. "Esri, where do they go? What do I tell them?"

He raises a hand to cut me off. "Chance, not here! You need to be in there. Bridge. Bridge, now!"

I look at Paul. He's scared. He's confused. He wants to help, but he has no answers beyond getting the others to that tunnel. I know that fear; I know that helplessness. I've felt it in hospitals. I've felt it in my bedroom with a pounding headache after a seizure. And I've seen it in others' faces. Mom's. Dad's.

My gate starts to light up. I glance at it and then to Paul's face. With a blink, I'm in the tunnel with the students. But no one knows I'm here.

"Esri?" I yell.

"Take them down the tunnel. Run. The next intersection, turn right."

I put my hand on Paul's shoulder. Again, I'm touching him, but not touching him. He doesn't feel anything. As the gate spins around my wrist, I feel instruction leaving my body and meeting Paul. I hear the sound of my voice: "Down the hall, Paul. The next intersection. Take a right."

"Come on, guys," Paul announces. "The way out is down here." Paul takes off running. The others follow. He runs, but not as fast as he can. His hand returns to his temple every five to ten steps. He awaits further instruction. I follow the group and keep my eyes focused on Paul. I try to keep my emotions in tune with his. He's terrified. He knows a powerful military is tracking him like prey. Waiting for directions from a voice only he can hear doesn't seem like a sustainable plan. Paul does everything he can to mask the panic that pulses through his veins. I use all my restraint not to scream for help from Esri. I'm not cut out for this.

"You have no choice," Esri's voice comes to me. "You're here. You must do what needs to be done. Moment by moment. Follow your brother, and guide him through this."

Paul reaches the first intersection. He turns right. He looks up after turning the corner. I hope for something promising. The look on Paul's face tells me there's more disappointment. A long hall leads to a dead end.

"Keep going," I hear Esri's voice.

"Go, Paul," I encourage. "We'll figure this out. One step at a time."

Paul glances over his shoulder at the others. He waves for them to continue following him.

"Paul, where are we going?" one of the students asks between breaths as they continue running. "It's a dead end down there."

"One step at a time," my heart tells Paul's.

"Just trust me, guys," Paul tries to assure them. "I got you out of the room, didn't I? We've got to keep going."

Paul picks up the pace. He runs towards the dead end. He accelerates like he's planning to bust through the concrete wall that looms in front of them. I worry about what will happen at the end. Will they continue to trust him? What will he say when they reach the wall? How can there possibly be another option?

"Up," I hear Esri's voice.

The glowing path that carries me through the bridge speeds in front of the running teenagers. I race in front of them and look up. I see a rusty ladder suspended about six feet from the floor. I rise and start to climb it, and somehow that message transfers to Paul. When he reaches the end of the tunnel, he too looks up. He jumps and grabs the first rung.

"Up here," he shouts. He pulls himself up and starts climbing the ladder. I look over my shoulder and continue to lead the way. It feels like he's following me. I guess he is. But not by sight. He knows to follow me because we're connected, connected like two people battling the same problem.

The ladder goes up for what feels like storys. It's rusted, but doesn't shake even as every student manages to clamber up from the floor.

I reach another dead end; this time we're cut off by the ceiling. The metal hatch above my head has a large round handle. It's what I imagine seals bank vaults.

"Esri?" I scream. No reply.

"Esri!" Nothing.

"Esri, we need some direction. None of us knows what's going on in here. What do we do?"

Paul rushes right through me like I'm a ghost. He grabs the handle. He grimaces as he uses all of his might to turn it to the right. It doesn't budge. He tries the other direction. No luck. He glances down at the student right below him on the ladder.

"Jane, grab that side of the handle," Paul says. "You pull up on that side while I push down on the other." Jane scrambles to balance on the top of the ladder next to Paul. The two try to open the hatch with no success.

"Maybe, it's the other way," Jane says. They try the reverse option. The handle remains stubbornly frozen.

They rest for a minute. They all do. I watch them clinging to the ladder and trying to catch their breaths, and I try to rationalize what's happening. Paul looks up at the hatch. The vertical tunnel falls silent except for the sound of heavy breathing. .

"Esri!" I yell.

"I'm here," I hear Esri's voice. It sounds dejected. "OK, what do we do?" I ask.

After a brief silence, he responds: "I don't know."

Panic rushes through my body. Paul feels it. He jumps a little, which catches Jane and the others by surprise.

"What do we do now, Paul?" she asks.

Paul's eyes meet Jane's. She reads his helplessness. Jane's head falls and she gazes down at the others below. Despair relays down the ladder. Despondent silence fills the tunnel.

Seconds later, a distant sound interrupts the quiet.

"Ssshh," one of the students at the bottom of the ladder instructs. "I think someone's coming."

The sound grows louder and more distinguishable. Boots stomp through the underground passageways. Someone barks orders at marching troops.

I turn my eyes back to the hatch. Paul follows suit. I examine everything I can see. To the right, I notice a keypad. It's not too different from the keypads in the room where I first found Paul.

"Hey, there's a keypad," Paul announces to the others. "I'll try the same code—"

Jane interrupts him: "What if it sets off an alarm or something? What if it's the wrong one. Won't it lead them directly to us?"

Paul turns to her. He doesn't know what to say to her legitimate concern. Angst climbs across the motionless bodies suspended on the rickety ladder. They look to Paul for their next steps, but he's just as uncertain as they are. I must do something.

I take a closer look at the keypad. To the right of the numbers, someone has scribbled a word: *Metis*.

What does *Metis* mean? It means something to somebody. I'm the only person around who can navigate to whoever wrote this and figure out what it means. I stare intently at the word and glance back and forth between it and the keypad. Surely the written word is associated with the keypad. Why else would someone have written it at the end of a tunnel next to a keypad that appears to be the only way out?

I sharpen my focus on the word. I consider what it could mean to the people running this experiment; the people trying to hide this place from the rest of the world. My wrist starts to warm. I look down and see my gate glowing.

I'm thrust out of the crowded tunnel. Then I'm navigating through an Unseen light tunnel. As I slow, the tunnel divides into two options. To the left, a snowy scene appears. To the right, I see what looks like Dr. Jacobs talking to a small group of people.

I move towards the scene with Dr. Jacobs and lean in. He speaks frantically: "I don't know how the subjects have escaped. They could not have aroused from their medically-induced comas without external influence. We must abandon this facility and relocate immediately. The transportation system is fully stocked with materials and ready to relocate to Metis."

There it is: *Metis.*

"What about the subjects?" a garbled voice asks. His face is out of the scene. "They've learned too much."

"We'll have to take that risk. Let the soldiers who have gone after them continue to search. If they don't succeed by the time we're ready to depart, we'll initiate facility self-destruct. It will flood the tunnels and terminate anyone left in the building."

My heart skips a beat. What kind of evil is this guy? He's willing to kill everybody just to cover this up. Who was he talking to?

As I ask that question, the scene zooms closer. I see who Dr. Jacbos is talking to.

General Palmer responds to Dr. Jacobs' suggestion: "Fair enough. Proceed to transportation for immediate transfer to Metis. Set the campus to self-destruct in fifteen minutes. We can't risk waiting any longer."

Two guards affirm his orders. Dr. Jacobs and General Palmer exit the room. The scene vanishes. I find myself back in the light tunnel. The snowy scene remains visible and available for me to approach. Not knowing what else to do, I move towards it.

"Metis," I say aloud. As if on command, the scene moves closer, and my gate illuminates. I look at my wrist and see a path into the scene light up. I cross it and find myself in a snowy desert. White snow and swirling wind surround me. The blinding blizzard calms for a moment and I see a single building. I make my way towards it. I notice it sits on the edge of a cliff, a frozen sea below it. The structure is half buried in snow. I look around, trying to figure out where I am. What does this place have to do with the word *Metis*? A heavily clothed person exits the building. He opens what looks like an electrical box on the front and begins flipping switches. There's a sign above the box. I move closer to see what it says. As I do, two words come into focus: *Project Metis*.

"This is where they're headed," I say. "But what does this have to do with the keypad back in the tunnels of the military base?"

I continue examining the sign for more clues. Below the word *Metis*, I see coordinates: 80 N, 99 E.

"That's it!" I yell. "It's the coordinates of the Metis building. That's the code. OK, what now?" I wrestle my racing mind to try to devise a plan. Paul. I have to get back to Paul. I have to navigate back to him immediately. I look at my wrist. It's shining.

"Paul!" I scream.

"Chance," Esri interrupts. "They're panicking. They're all yelling at each other. The students voted to use the code that got them out of the room. It didn't work. Alarms are going off. They need the coordinates. Get to them. Get to them."

"How?" I yell.

"You know how!" Esri rebukes. "They're panicking. Panicking!"

I squeeze my eyes shut. I think of Paul and the only time I've seen him panic. It was the first time he was alone with me when I had an episode. He thought I had died because my face had turned blue and he couldn't get me to wake up. I dive deep into that memory. I try to embrace the helplessness Paul felt that day. I feel the tunnel wrap itself around me. I don't want to open my eyes. I'm scared. It feels liking keeping them closed will help.

I know the navigation and bridge have completed when I hear teenage voices arguing with each other.

"We should have never followed you!" one yells.

"Guys, calm down, we need to work together," Paul pleads.

Once I hear Paul's voice, I start to repeat the coordinates over and over again.

"8099.

"8099.

"8099.

"8099."

The blaring alarm screams through the halls. Thundering boots gain ground on the kids. They're close.

I narrow in on Paul. I hear my voice: "Paul, it's 8099." Paul turns from the others. He looks at the keypad. He raises his hand and enters the code.

A thundering clunk stops the arguing. It echoes down the tunnel, nearly overpowering the noise of approaching boots. Faces turn to

Paul. He grips the handle and easily turns it counterclockwise. He pushes the hatch open and peers into the night sky. Relief washes across his face. I fall away from the scene back into the Unseen. I'm back in a globe of light watching Paul and the others from a distance.

Exhaustion weighs heavily on me. I start to lose touch with the now freed classmates. I see Paul direct them out. He holds the hatch open until each one has left. When the last student makes it out, Paul drops the hatch. He turns the handle to secure it. He looks around in weary bewilderment.

He knows he's heard my voice, but he has no idea how.

"I don't really understand it myself, Paul," I say to myself. "But you heard me, and you listened. That's what matters. You did it. I did it. We did it."

The vision of Paul fades to black, and then even that fades away. I lay in the warm afternoon air of the Seen world. My dead weight rests like a wet towel stuck to the treehouse floor.

Paul escaped. Mission complete. And, then I remember...Dad.

Chapter 23

"**D**ad!"

I try to jump off the treehouse floor, but my body aches. Exhaustion traps me. My heart begins to race. Bridging in the Unseen has taken a greater toll on my body today than it has on any previous trip.

"You're not done," I preach to myself. "Dad's not safe."

General Palmer and Dr. Jacobs have started their escape by now. They agreed to destroy the facility. Dad and everyone in the building, even their own troops, are about to die. I have to do something. I must get back in there.

Lying on my back, I stare at the treehouse ceiling. I try to drum up thoughts of Dad and his desire to save his son and to right the wrongs of this project.

Nothing.

I beg the stars to come. I urge my nerves to warm. I clench my fists, grit my teeth, and worry. I worry as much as I can. I have never wanted to feel pre-seizure symptoms, but at this moment, I'd welcome them like a gift.

Nothing.

My energy is fully depleted. Helplessness pins my body to the floor. My mind races. I struggle to consider my next move. Before I conjure up the first steps of any plan, a scream from inside the house interrupts my thoughts.

It's Mom. Has she heard from Dad? I pull myself to the treehouse entrance and try to lower myself to the ground. I can barely grip the rungs. My legs are useless to bear weight. I fall the entire distance from treehouse to the ground. With a flop, I collapse to the worn patch of dusty lawn under the treehouse. From here, I peer into the back window and see Mom's face pouring tears. They aren't the tears of fear and despair that she's fought back day after day. They're tears of happiness.

She's elated. I haven't seen such emotion out of her since...since, I can't remember when. Her face beams joy, relief, disbelief, and love all at once. The sight of my mother rescued from her demons is enough to jolt some energy back into my body.

I push myself to my feet and stumble to the house. I enter, and Mom's voice matches her face. Her tone rings thankful.

"Where are you now, Paul?" she asks. "Did your father and General Palmer find you?"

She waits for a response. Her brow turns. Paul's response has confused her.

"What do you mean you've escaped? Are you not with General Palmer then?"

The ease in her voice turns to concern again. Then the helplessness that has defined this summer thunders back into the house.

"But—" Paul interrupts her with something. He's trying to assure her that he and the others are OK, but he's having trouble doing so. She has no idea what kind of madness he's trapped in. And Paul has no idea that the whole facility is about to flood in self-destruction.

I need to talk to him.

As Paul tries to ease Mom's mind, her eyes catch a glimpse of me. She mouths the words *it's Paul* and gives a forced thumbs up. She's back in *protect Chance from the truth* mode. She doesn't want me stressed out by Paul's and Dad's predicament.

I need to talk to him. "Can I talk to him?" I ask. I need to talk to him.

"Just a minute, Paul," Mom interrupts him. "Chance's just walked in." She turns to me with a fake pleasantness, "Chance, it's Paul. He's safe. Now we're just going to figure out where Dad is and get them both back here. OK, sound good? Now why don't you run upstairs to your room and get some downtime. You'll want to be fully rested to spend time with Paul and Dad when they get home."

I need to talk to him.

"Yeah, that's great Mom," I say. "Can I just talk to him for a second though? It would be great to hear his voice."

"Not just yet, Chance. We have some things we need to figure out quickly so we can make sure he gets home safe and sound."

I don't move. I don't know what to say. The fifteen minutes

before the facility floods tick away as I wait.

I need to talk to him.

Mom returns to Paul. She turns away from me and walks across the room to get some distance between us. Maybe she thinks I'll lose interest or at least not hear the serious tone of the conversation that's inevitably coming.

"OK, hon," Mom continues. "What are you seeing around you right now? Maybe I can get a hold of your Dad. He's with the General, so they can't be too far away."

I need to talk to him.

I quietly creep across the kitchen floor behind Mom. I slip my hand over her shoulder and yank the phone out of her hand.

"Chance!" she yells.

"Paul, it's me. I know you heard me earlier. Hear me now. Dad is in there. The whole place is going to flood. Get him out!"

"Chance!" Mom yells again. She grabs the phone out of my hand. "What are you doing? And what are you talking about? Please, let us figure this out. Go to your room, now! Get some rest. I'll be up to check on you in a second. I know you're excited to see Paul, but we have some final things to figure out. Go! Now!"

"Yeah," I say. "Good. I'll just go to bed. Sorry. I guess I'm just excited. I needed to hear his voice. Sorry." She hasn't processed what I said or the fact that I didn't even hear Paul's voice, but Paul heard the message, and that's the best I can do.

Mom continues talking to Paul. I leave the room. With the heat of the moment now passed, sluggishness overwhelms my body once again. One step at a time, I shuffle up the stairs. I stop telling my legs what to do. They remember the path to my bedroom on their own. My arms instinctively close the door as I step onto the familiar carpet. I collapse on my mattress.

My body argues with itself. My aching bones and muscles beg for sleep. My worrying mind keeps me awake wondering if Paul will make it to Dad. Do I need to get back into the Unseen? Can he do it without me? I'm not so sure.

I hear footsteps coming up the stairs. Mom's coming in to check on me. I roll away from the door and pretend to be asleep. She enters. I hope she'll see me sleeping and leave. Instead, she sits on the edge of the bed. She rubs my back and hums a gentle song. She pauses every once in a while to choke back the now returned tears of sadness. Will she ever leave? Despite my exhaustion, I'm getting restless. The more I pretend to be asleep, the more awake I become. My mind is winning the battle over my body's exhaustion. I need to get back to the Unseen and figure out what's going on. Unlike before, I can help now. That I know.

I reach my breaking point in frustration. I can't lie here faking sleep for much longer. Finally Mom bends over me and kisses my forehead. "Rest easy, Chance," she whispers. I hold my breath and wait for her to leave the room. The door squeaks and finally clicks shut. I shoot up.

I need to get back in. I squeeze my fists. A noise at the window interrupts me. I turn to look. It's Esri.

"Shall we?" he asks. "Let's go," I reply.

Chapter 24

Esri and I enter the Unseen together. He pays little attention to me and gets straight to work.

He's not looking to teach me anything. He doesn't ask me to navigate. That doesn't disappoint me. My energy is zapped. I don't bother trying to get off the black floor where I sit. Seen or Unseen, I have little energy to give. I feel useless to anyone. My eyes waver from open to closed uncontrollably. Each time they open, I see a fresh sort of navigation tunnel. Esri brings a new level of focus to this trip. The tunnels display his concentration. I sit in wonder and watch the omnituen masterfully maneuver through his Unseen world.

Eventually, separate beams of glowing colors meld into a single cylinder of soft light. We race through it at an incalculable speed. I force my head up to take in the experience. I feel wind on my face. I expect a scene to appear at the end of the tunnel. Soon enough, it does.

A singular image gathers at the end of the tunnel. A shimmer of hope rises in my chest. I wait to see Paul or Dad or maybe both.

I try to get up, but I can't move my legs. I look up at Esri. He extends a hand. I grab it, and he pulls me to my feet.

"Is it—"

"Shh," Esri cuts me off. "Not yet."

The scene slowly comes into focus. At first, I see nothing but a single person wearing a hospital gown. The body is moving. It's running across a dusty field. It has to be Paul.

"Paul?" I ask. I look at Esri. He remains focused on the scene, but nods his head to confirm my suspicion.

"You've got this, Paul," I say, wishing he could hear me.

The scene clears up. Paul runs like he's fleeing a disaster. When I see his destination, I realize he isn't running away from anything. Instead, he's rushing straight towards a catastrophe. He must have left the others somewhere beyond the perimeter of the base because he's alone. He runs back to the building with a look of reckless devotion across his face. Unarmed, uninformed, and running out of energy, Paul approaches one of the most sinister government compounds mankind has ever created. And he's moving as fast as possible.

He clearly received my message over the phone. He's going back in to get Dad.

Paul slows as he reaches a side door. No guards await him. They must be in the tunnels, or maybe they have already abandoned the base. Paul, now familiar with the locking system, locates a keypad to the side of the gate.

"Chance?" Esri questions. "You'll need to bridge to get him the code."

"He's got this," I say.

"Pardon?" Esri asks. "Chance, I know you are tired, but—"

"Just watch," I say.

Esri and I turn back to the scene. Paul enters 0423. The door opens letting out a blast of the still-blaring alarm. Although he hasn't found Dad yet, and his chances of doing so seem pretty slim, I'm more than proud of my brother. His courage and strength give me a newfound energy. I stand like a diehard fan cheering on my favorite team.

Paul runs down a long hallway until he comes to a junction. He looks at signs on the wall and overhead. He evaluates the options to his right, his left, and then continues down the hall in front of him. He hesitates.

"Chance," Esri prompts me.

"Hold on," I say. "Give him a second."

I don't know what Paul read, but he decides to go left, and chooses with conviction. He bolts down another hallway. Esri doesn't say anything. I take that to mean Paul chose correctly.

"Come on, Paul. You've got this," I say.

Paul comes to another stop at the end of a hall. This time, he has to choose left or right. He looks back and forth between the options. The hall falls silent. The alarm that has continued since Paul first set his classmates free has finally stopped. The silence paralyzes Paul. It does the same to me.

"The tunnels, they'll start to flood," Esri says. So much has happened in the fifteen minutes since General Palmer ordered the facility's destruction; I can hardly believe we're only just now running out of time.

The sound of sprinklers coming to life interrupts the silence. Water sprays from the tunnel ceilings surrounding Paul. Paul looks panicked. I squeeze my fists in reflex.

"Chance," says Esri. "We can't rely on good guesses now. Those halls will flood quickly, and Paul needs to know exactly where he's going. He must go right and then take the third hall on the left. Your father will be in a room down that hall, last door on the left."

Before Esri finishes his instructions, I begin my bridge. Paul understands the stake. There's no place for that water to go. It's going to fill up. But nothing will stop him from trying to find Dad. I know it. I focus on the fear of drowning and the drive to save Dad. My wrist lights up. I glance down at it. It glows violent shades of red. I turn my eyes back to Paul. He remains frozen stiff. He knows he has to make a decision quickly, and it must be the correct decision. There's no time for second chances.

I intensify my focus. The frame around the scene fades. I cross into the hall and stand next to Paul. I swear I can feel his heavy breathing. Can that be true?

Without saying a word, I start running in the direction Esri instructed. I hear my voice fill the tunnel without me verbalizing a single word: "Follow me, Paul."

Paul starts after me. I run faster, pushing my Unseen body to its limit. He matches my pace. We reach the first turn. The water is already ankle deep.

I turn, and I hear my voice again: "This way." Paul turns, and we run on. We pass the first two lefts. The water rises to mid-shin, and Paul is struggling to keep up his speed in the dark liquid. I turn at the third left. My voice booms throughout the hallway: "Keep coming."

I see Dad's door ahead of me. I glance over my shoulder. Paul is right behind me. I slow as I approach the door. Somehow my heart beats even faster. I stop and fearfully peer through the protected glass in the steel door. There he is.

"Dad!" I yell.

Paul arrives.

"Dad!" Paul screams.

Dad jumps off the chair where he had been crouching and avoiding the water that rains down from a sprinkler overhead . His face goes from startled fear to tearful joy when he realizes who it is.

"Paul," Dad gasps. I've never seen tears flow so freely from Dad's eyes. He runs to the door and spreads his hand on the glass. Paul puts his hand on the other side. They stare at each other with a contentment and relief that deserves to last much longer. But there isn't time.

"We've got to get you out of there, Dad," Paul says. "They've started to flood the halls." I glance down to see the water already up to Paul's knees.

Paul looks to the side of the door. A keypad is there as he has come to expect. He punches in 0423.

Nothing happens.

He punches it in again, this time more slowly. Nothing happens.

"Dad, the code isn't working," Paul says. "Is there a keypad on your side?"

Dad searches around. "I don't see anything," he replies.

I back against the hallway wall. "Esri?" I ask. I look at the water rising on Paul. It has cleared his knees and brushes the bottom of his flimsy hospital gown.

"Esri!" I scream.

Paul yanks a fire extinguisher off the wall and starts smashing it into the door window. Dad lets him try three or four times before he stops Paul.

"I've tried that on this side, Paul," he says. "It didn't work. It's too strong."

"OK, OK." Paul says, still sounding resilient. "We'll figure this out. Let me try one more code."

Paul grabs his head. "What was that code?"

"The coordinates!" I yell. "Esri, what were the coordinates?"

"8099," I hear Esri's voice.

For the second time, I start yelling the coordinates over and over again. Paul punches them in.

Nothing happens.

"What do we do, Esri?" I ask. He doesn't respond right away. I fear his silence is another indication that he doesn't know what to tell me.

Paul stares at Dad through the glass, and Dad back at Paul. The water continues to rise.

"We can't stop now," I say.

"We can't stop now, Dad," Paul echoes out loud. "We've got to get him out," I say.

"Let's get you out of there, Dad," Paul says.

I join Paul by the door. I slam my shoulder against the door. I slam it again. And again. I'm not physically in the room, but I feel the dull pain eating away at my arm and shoulder, sharpening with each blow.

Paul starts to slam his shoulder in the door as well. He slams it again. And again. We hit the door over and over with increasing intensity. Our minds and wills unite in effort while our physical bodies are hundreds of miles away from each other.

Our shoulders pound the door. The water rises to our thighs.

"Come on!" I scream. "Just budge!"

"Come on! Come on! Come on!" Paul screams. The water hits my waist.

"It's OK, Paul!" Dad tries to interrupt. "It's OK, you've done your best. You need to get out of here now!"

"No!" Paul and I yell.

In complete defiance of Dad's suggestion to leave him behind, we expel the last bit of energy we have.

"Paul, listen to me, Son. Save yourself." One more slam. The door pops open.

I collapse into the water. Paul falls into Dad's arms. All three of us, in tears of matched joy and exhaustion, have only a moment to catch our breaths before I hear Esri's voice.

"There's another escape hatch, Chance," he says. "It's at the end of this hallway. It's labeled *Metis*. It should take the same code."

I push my Unseen feet to the floor and start towards the hall, leaving Dad and Paul behind. I don't have the breath to call out, but the tunnel fills with my voice: "This way, Paul. Come on."

"Dad, that way," Paul says and points.

"Do you know the way out?" Dad asks Paul. "Ah...yes," says Paul.

I trudge through the waist-high water. Perplexed why I feel water when I'm not really here, I struggle through. Dad and Paul do the same, following me. At the end of the hall, a ladder leads up to a hatch just like the one where Paul set the others free. I climb the ladder and see the word *Metis* scribbled.

I wait until Paul and Dad climb the ladder. Paul's eyes go straight to the keypad.

I start repeating the coordinates as fast as I can, over and over again.

"8099.

"8099.

"8099."

I remain in the scene, but everything begins to blur. Paul must have entered the code, because I hear the hatch click. When it slams shut, I find myself lying limp next to Esri in a navigation tunnel.

I've lost complete control of my Unseen body. I guess that means I've lost control of my mind. I compulsively continue to mumble the coordinates:

"8099...8099...8099."

"Chance, it's alright," I hear Esri say. I can't see him clearly. Dark spots overtake my field of vision. "They got out. You can stop saying the code."

I can't get the numbers out of my mind. My mouth keeps saying the words. The *Metis* sign post won't leave me alone. It's seared into my mind's eye. There's no escape.

"Chance, stop," Esri says.

I don't stop. The tunnel lights up. "Chance, no. We don't want to go there now. You need to get back home and get some rest."

It's too late. We're already on our way. Esri grabs my wrist. I don't know if he's trying to counter my navigation or what, but he's trying something. We pick up speed.

Esri fights against me, and colors start to lose their tunnel shape. Beams of light fracture off like sparks from a braking train. The blues and greens turn to grays and shades of black.

"Chance, stop! Now!"

I hear another voice. It isn't Esri's, but I've heard it before.

"Yes, do stop, Mr. Chance," Scab says in his sarcastic tone. "You don't have any business visiting this place. And do you really need to be taught another lesson?"

The lights dim. The three of us come to a stop in blackness.

"What do you want, Scab?" Esri asks.

"Oh, nothing. I've no use for either of you. I merely want you to leave this place. What interest could you have in the middle of an ice desert anyway?"

"We'll go," Esri concedes. That doesn't seem like Esri, but I haven't the energy nor the wits to contest.

"Good," Scab says. "Glad we all agree on something."

Esri picks me up off the ground and turns away from Scab. I look down at his wrist, which glows intensely. In a flash, Esri turns around and the tunnel instantly surrounds us. We flash past a scowling Scab. I don't remember ever traveling so fast in the Unseen.

Bolts of red lightning blow past our ears as we travel. Scab is coming after us.

"Stop, now!" I hear him scream in the distance.

We come to a scene. It's the same building covered in snow that we'd previously seen. A vehicle pulls up to the building. The image comes into clear view. A car door opens. Out steps an armed man. He looks like a guard. Two more follow him: General Palmer and Dr. Jacobs.

Before we can react, thunder cracks and Esri screams in pain.

I turn to him. A red bolt of sustained electrical current strikes his back. I follow the fizzing red glow with my tired eyes and see that the bolt originates at Scab's hand.

Esri turns to me. He grabs my wrist. "Go!" he screams. He releases my wrist with a pull. My world goes black. The next light I see is on my bedroom ceiling, a fan spinning around it.

Chapter 25

The sun splits through my bedroom curtains. It singes my eyes when they crack open. The tiniest ray shoots needles into my brain. I haven't had a headache like this since... since my last seizure. Did I have a seizure? Is that why I feel so bad? How long have I been asleep? I wonder if this entire summer... the Unseen, Esri, the project...has it all been a seizure-induced dream?

If it were all a dream or some side effect of seizures, that means Paul was never captured, Dad never went after him, and my family should be downstairs together enjoying a *normal* summer break.

I jump out of bed to see if anyone is around. That was a mistake. The headache grips my brain and squeezes it until my stomach churns. I run to the bathroom. I puke for what seems like hours. When surely nothing is left in my system, I flush the toilet and collapse on the floor. My lungs pump in and out, recovering. Each inhale sends ringing to my ears.

I lie on the cool bathroom floor and concentrate on not puking. My breath calms and slows. I hear footsteps coming up the stairs along with Mom's voice. She's talking to someone. The tone of her voice is upbeat. There's no trace of hopelessness.

Maybe it was all a dream.

I grip the sink counter and pull myself to a seated position. If she comes in, I don't want her to see me lying on the floor. That will freak her out, and my head can't handle that right now.

I hear her grab the doorknob, but she doesn't come straight in. She's talking on the phone, and the conversation isn't over. I listen intently.

"What do you mean, they don't know where they are?" she asks.

She waits for an explanation and then says, "That just doesn't make sense. That place must have cameras everywhere." Another pause and then, "OK, so you guys are how far away now?"

It sounds like Dad and Paul are on the other end of the call. Are they coming back from a top secret military base, or just an insignificant errand?

"Oh, that close? Great. We'll see you two soon."

The conversation nears a close. If I make it back to bed, I might avoid inquiry as to how I'm feeling. I rush on all fours to the bed. I crawl back onto the mattress and under the covers.

Mom turns the knob and opens the door slowly. "Chance? Are you awake?"

I roll over towards her. I don't need to *act* tired. I'm still utterly worn out. Puking only made it worse.

"Sort of," I say.

"Good," she says. "I have good news, Chance." "What's that?"

"Your father and Paul. They'll be here shortly. We'll finally have that summer you had hoped for?"

I question myself again. Had it all been in my head: the school invasion, Esri, the Unseen, everything?

"That's great Mom. When will they be back?"

"I just got off the phone with Dad," she says. "They'll be here any minute."

"Good. I'll go ahead and get dressed." I'm still wearing my clothes from this morning, but after three trips to the Unseen, falling out the treehouse, and now my time in the bathroom, I could use a fresh set.

"Good," she says. Mom starts to leave my room, and I'm still confused about reality. She pauses before closing the door behind her. "They better get home quick. The President addresses the nation in half an hour."

"About what?" I ask.

"Updates about the program. Obviously it didn't go as planned. Your father and Paul said that they can't find Dr. Jacobs or General Palmer anywhere. Recordings from the base have been wiped. The whole place is destroyed. Sounds like this is just the beginning of a bigger mess. But at least our Paul and Dad are home."

It was real. It was all real.

"There they are," Mom says. She turns and runs down the stairs. I jump out of bed. My stomach rumbles, but I ignore it. I pull on clean pants and a shirt and follow Mom down the stairs. Everything turns to a blur. I'm rushing towards my family, but my field of vision distorts. Words and household noises jumble together. When things finally clear up, we're all together—all four of us—in a group hug. No words. Plenty of tears.

We stay in our family huddle for ten seconds, or maybe ten minutes. Maybe ten hours. We're finally together, and that's what matters to me. It's what matters to all of us.

At some point, Mom breaks the moment. "Well, the President is about to come on," she says. "Let's see what he has to say about this mess you boys created." She turns to Paul and Dad and smiles. Man, it is good to see her smile.

She turns on the television. We all sit down on our favorite seats in the den and wait to see what the President will say.

I've seen the *Stay tuned for a special announcement from the President of the United States of America* notice on the television before. The last few times it's triggered the most unsettling weeks of my life. My brain remembers. Shivers dance down my spine. My nerves start to heat up. But now, I know the purpose of those nerves. They're nothing more than an ability to channel enough energy to move from the Seen to the Unseen. It's not the disability this world has come to label it. It's an innate gift. I only needed some help learning how to understand it. I wiggle my fingers, and my nerves cool off. The screen switches to an empty podium which is soon filled by the President.

"Citizens of America,

"I stand before you today filled with two polar opposite emotions. On one hand, I'm thrilled to announce that the students that were recently drafted and taken into top secret military custody for the purpose of initiating self- directed evolutionary techniques are all safe. They are in the process of being reunited with their families, and none of the students were harmed or exposed to the experimental techniques originally announced.

"On the other hand, I am disappointed, saddened, and ashamed to announce that two Americans, the leaders of this project, will go down in history as some of the greatest traitors in our nation's existence, and are, at this time unfortunately still at large.

"General Palmer and Dr. Jacobs, who originally addressed this nation from this podium alongside me, have escaped the military facility where the project was conducted. In their escape, they initiated a self- destructive device on the facility, which is now destroyed. In doing so, they abandoned support teams and the project participants and left them to perish. Unfortunately, some of our brave and selfless military men and women have died in this tragedy. Thankfully, the project participants were able to escape the facility before the self destruction event concluded.

"As for General Palmer and Dr. Jacobs, we do not know where they are. We do not know what their intentions are. However, we have reason to believe that they have not abandoned their nefarious mission. We don't know what that mission is, but we know it to be dangerous towards the United States of America and its citizens.

"We will keep the public informed as necessary. If you become aware of any information on either man, please immediately contact law enforcement. Again, we thank the men and women who gave their lives at the project facility, and are grateful for the safe return of project participants. We will not rest until we bring these two enemies of the US to justice."

The screen goes black.

"Where did they go?" Mom asks. She turns to Dad. "I don't know. No one we've talked to knows."

At that moment, Paul and I turn to each other. We don't say a word, but we both know what I'm thinking: "I know where they are."

"Well, I'm just glad we're all safe and home," Mom says. "Right?"

"Right," Dad confirms. He gathers the three of us together for one more bear hug and then asks, "Who's hungry? I'm starved." He heads towards the kitchen. Mom follows.

Paul and I stay in the den for a moment. I don't know what to say. His face tells me he doesn't either. I'm equally thrilled to have him physically in front of me and terrified of what this new normal will mean for us going forward.

Paul reaches out and hugs me. He squeezes me hard. Through tears, I mumble, "I was—"

"I know," he says. "I don't know how, but I know."

"I love you, Paul."

"I love you, Chance. We'll figure it out. We always do."

The End